CRITICAL ACCLAIM FOR *CRIME UNDER THE SUN*

"It may be a cliché to say an anthology has something for all readers, but *Crime Under the Sun* delivers in full. From cozy and quirky to gimlet-eyed and hard-boiled and with more than a couple of sides of tense and chilling. Story to story, I was delighted, thrilled, amused, and amazed."

—Art Taylor, Edgar Award-winning author of
The Adventure of the Castle Thief
and Other Expeditions and Indiscretions

"The Golden State has a dark underside in *Crime Under the Sun*, a lively and varied compendium of murder, mayhem, bad choices, and bad dreams. Seedy noir to whimsical cozy, and caper plot to psychological drama, the anthology offers an assortment of vengeful malcontents, ingenious professionals and hapless wannabes, plus few decent souls. Sharp characterization, smooth prose, and some echoes of old time Hollywood's tarnished glamor complete an entertaining package."

—Janice Law, author of the Francis Bacon mysteries

"A scorching selection of crime stories that will leave you dying for more."

—Stephen D. Rogers, author of *Shot to Death*

"Whoever wrote 'there's nothing new under the sun' obviously hasn't read *Crime Under the Sun*, in which the San Diego chapter of Sisters in Crime offers up fifteen stories that are not only new but noteworthy. Readers may not be familiar with all of the contributors, some of whom are early in their writing careers—but you're sure to be seeing more of them!"

—Josh Pachter, editor of the Anthony Award finalist *Paranoia Blues: Crime Fiction Inspired by the Songs of Paul Simon*

"A lovely collection of criminous tales, delightfully diverse in style, featuring work by some of the best writers producing short fiction today."

—Tom Mead, author of *Death and the Conjuror* and *The Murder Wheel*

"*Crime Under the Sun* features a collection of twists, jagged edges, one-two punches and crisp storytelling from sunny California. With endearing protagonists, villains you love to hate, some cool characters coming off the page and murder mysteries galore, this collection showcases great talent."

—Ryan Sayles, author of *Like Whitewashed Tombs*

CRIME UNDER THE SUN

PARTNERS IN CRIME,
THE SAN DIEGO CHAPTER OF
SISTERS IN CRIME ANTHOLOGIES

Crossing Borders
Crime Under the Sun

MATT COYLE, NAOMI HIRAHARA,
AND TAMMY KAEHLER, EDITORS

CRIME UNDER THE SUN

A SISTERS IN CRIME ANTHOLOGY

Down & Out Books
3959 Van Dyke Road, Suite 265
Lutz, FL 33558
DownAndOutBooks.com

Cover design by Partners in Crime, the San Diego Chapter of Sisters in Crime

ISBN: 1-64396-322-8
ISBN-13: 978-1-64396-322-8

TABLE OF CONTENTS

FOREWORD

Catriona McPherson

If we think of Southern California, what comes to mind is a perfect climate, a glittering ocean, pristine beaches, and fun, fun, fun, fun, fun.

So, of course, when fifteen mystery authors set stories there, what we end up with is dirty work, old scores, flawed plans, dark secrets, unlucky breaks, and heartrendingly small dreams that still prove too big.

Just how we like it.

Crime Under the Sun is the second anthology offered by Partners in Crime, the San Diego chapter of Sisters in Crime. You—most fortunate reader—will meet a beguiling bail bondswoman hanging onto the family business by her fingernails, a magnificent old coot bound to his land and his cattle, four all-too-believable teens playing a deadly game, a knight in tarnished armor getting crafty at a ball game, and a kick-ass eleven-year-old cowgirl who takes on a real-life mystery from Hollywood's Golden Age.

California life is laid bare: revelations about just how much the journey-time on the 101 can be squeezed to take care of business en route to the airport; news that an iconic hotdog can be *too* appetizing; and confirmation that Tinseltown's underbelly has an underbelly, grim and poignant in equal measure.

To play the "it's my intro and I'll say what I want to" card briefly, I'm going to float the notion that, as a town isn't a town without a bookshop, an anthology isn't an anthology without a biblio-mystery. And here we get a creepy old mansion thrown in with the librarians too.

It's less idiosyncratic to declare that the best mystery anthologies should embrace the whole of our beloved genre and *Crime Under the Sun* has nailed it. We've got a cipher to decode in a tale of high stakes in the tech world, a doomed brush between a femme fatale and an ordinary joe close to snapping, a crisp, clever procedural featuring a world-weary cop in a world with a lot to weary her, metafictional fun for readers (although the laughter of writers in edit-mode might be strained), a little gem of a story where obsession becomes fatally clouded judgment on the corner of home-improvement and noir. And the uncoziest cat tale ever.

Enjoy!

SHOOTING FOR THE STARS

Michelle Rodenborn

The trailer door swung open, the noonday sun laying bare the shuttered room.

Freddy Rollins squinted in the glare as Jenny sashayed in. Red hair blazing. Miles of leg. Tanzanite eyes skewering his.

"You." He bit his cheek. "You were supposed to stay gone."

She slammed the door shut. "We got unfinished business."

He sat behind an oversized desk, presiding over bowls of weed, scales, and bags of colored pills. Eugene, his beefy right-hand man, sprawled in the chair before him, staring at Jenny.

"Hey, Eugene." She flashed him a white smile.

Rollins studied her, stroking his stubble beard. "You and me are all settled up."

Her mouth shot open, but he silenced her with a flick of his hand.

He turned to Eugene, tossing him a list of names. "Make these dopers pay up. And don't take no trade, like you did before. No TVs. No jewelry. No piece-of-shit car. You got that, Fat Man?"

Eugene rose slowly and shoved the list into his pocket. "Got it. Cash only."

Jenny's startling eyes followed Eugene out the door, then she planted herself in front of the desk, hands on hips.

"Where's the rest of the money, Freddy? I'm not stupid. I know you got more than twenty grand."

He met her stare. “You got the same ten thou I got.”

She scoffed. “Don’t lie to me. I heard you on the phone, hitting them up for more.”

A long pause. He balled his fists below the desk to keep from grabbing her white throat. “You spied on me?”

She plopped into Eugene’s chair, a hint of a smile lifting her face. “It wasn’t spying. I came back to The Oceanaire to get my things and heard you yelling from the next room.”

He felt an itch rise in his blood, the way it did when his girls got out of line. Jenny had been trouble from the get-go—she never knew her place.

“Once I get my cut, I’m out of your hair.” She leaned forward, splaying her hands on the desk. “I need a lot more than ten grand to get set up in Hollywood.”

He snorted. “Gonna be a big star, are you?”

He came around to the front of the desk, sat at its edge, stretched out his legs. “You got your share, Jenny, same as me.”

Her red lips drew back like she’d smelled something rotten. “Don’t you try to cheat me.”

Lifting her chin, she jabbed a thumb at her chest. “I’m the one had to do the jerk. Was me took all the risk getting that video. You didn’t do sh—.”

“Enough!” Rollins jumped to his feet, waves of heat engulfing his body.

All his girls owed him, especially Jenny. It was his idea to scam the senator. He made the man pay up. If Jenny thought she’d see more of the cash, she had another think coming.

He stood over her, fists clenched at his sides, watching her face grow pale.

She touched his arm gently. “Sorry, Freddy. But I’m desperate for money. There’s a double deposit on this apartment I found. And I need acting lessons, workshops, professional photos...none of it’s cheap.”

He chuckled low, watching her mouth tremble and eyes fill with tears. Jenny was quite the actress already.

He pulled a Marlboro from a pack on the desk, lit it, then moved behind her chair. Cigarette dangling from his mouth, he brushed her hair to one side and stroked her neck.

She flinched. “Business first.”

Rollins smiled to himself, a different fantasy in mind. He gave her neck a last good squeeze, leaving imprints on her skin.

He went to the fridge and grabbed a bottle of beer. As he twisted off the top, she raised her voice—that high, whiny one that scraped up his spine.

“Fair’s fair, Freddy. How much more did you get?”

A box with the remains of last night’s pizza stared at him from the sink. He tossed the bottle cap on top and downed half the beer.

Wiping his mouth with the back of his hand, he chose his words. “Nothing yet. I meet their guy this afternoon.”

“How much you asking?”

He watched the faucet drip, calculating his lie. “Another twenty.”

Jenny’s mouth fell open. “That’s all? We got a buck-naked U.S. senator on tape, snorting coke and fucking a pro. The tabloids would pay big-time for that.”

He lanced her with a look. “Don’t even think about the tabloids.”

She came up to him quickly, her voice breathy, wheedling. “But why not? A lawyer I know says we could make a bun—.”

He slammed his beer on the counter. “You told someone what we did?”

She backed up a step. “Calm down, Freddy. I left it…hypothetical. He doesn’t know the senator’s name.”

Blood pounded in his ears—the conniving bitch.

After her date with the senator, Jenny had stopped by his trailer, as planned. She’d handed over the sports watch-spy cam he’d bought for the occasion, the memory card still inside. But she must’ve copied the video first, then later shared it with some hack.

And was stupid enough to let on what she'd done.

He kept his eyes on her as he took a long drag on the cigarette and blew smoke at the ceiling. "You think it's smart to double-cross the senator? His men play rough."

She crossed her arms and pushed back her shoulders. "I think the senator pays what that tape's worth—or he gets what he deserves."

Up close, her eyes lost much of their intensity and whatever faint intelligence it implied. They looked vacant now, unable to hold his gaze. Only vanity behind them.

To think this nitwit might foul up his biggest score ever.

He checked his watch. "Meet me back here at six and we'll split the pot. We can discuss your lawyer friend then."

She wore a smug, satisfied smile that he ached to erase.

He raised his brows. "Meantime, you could hightail it to The Oceanaire—squeeze in some work to pay for those acting lessons."

Her upper lip twitched in a sneer. "You just gotta dis everyone, doncha? Even Eugene, who does everything for you."

His steam rose like a kettle about to blow.

He grabbed the beer bottle and downed the rest of the brew, giving his heat time to cool. Then, plastering on a smile, he led her to the door.

"See you at six."

Jenny waited outside Freddy's trailer, one of five rental units set back from a noisy West L.A. street. No sign announced the ramshackle property. You could drive right by and never notice it was there.

Now an hour past sunset, chilly ocean gusts whipped her hair and slapped her legs. She pulled her jacket tight. Her insides quaked, but not from the cold.

She'd followed Freddy to the meet-up with the senator's man, then back to the trailer. He'd gone inside briefly, returning with a shovel he took to his backyard.

Peeking from behind the vacant unit next door, she'd watched him shove aside a boulder and dig a hole. He'd pulled two cloth sacks from inside his jacket, buried them, and replaced the stone.

Minutes later, he'd hopped into his car and driven off, leaving her free to find the hundred and fifty thousand dollars hidden inside those bags. Too bad she'd needed her new man's help moving the boulder—or she would've kept it all for herself.

It nearly made her sick, trusting her guy with all that money. But it wasn't safe to keep it with her for the meeting with Freddy.

She'd waited nearby the trailer court in case he came home early and checked on his stash. She couldn't let that happen—Freddy would kill her once he learned what she'd done.

Pacing in front of the trailer, she reviewed her plan. Freddy always underestimated her and wouldn't see it coming. It would look like a drug deal gone bad.

And chances were good no one would hear the gunshot—or bother to report it.

Of the five trailers, only two were occupied. Freddy's sole neighbor, a war vet with PTSD, drank all day and rarely stepped outside. Likely, he'd be passed out or too drunk to care.

And even if someone called 9-1-1, she'd be long gone before the police showed up.

She reached inside her purse for the cold comfort of her .38 Special. Afterward, she'd wipe her prints from the gun and ditch it. Though the cops couldn't trace it to her, anyway.

The revolver had belonged to a john who hit her one time too many. She'd taken it from his jacket pocket—after running a switchblade across his throat.

Her heart thundered as Freddy's beater entered the drive. Taking deep breaths, she watched him park and get out.

The sight of him brought on a cold sweat.

He brushed past her and opened his door. "Missed you at The Oceanaire."

She followed him in on shaky legs. "I was packing my apartment."

"Good. Got you more Hollywood money."

He dropped his scuffed leather briefcase on the desk, his back to her.

"All I could get was another ten. Here's your half."

He turned around, a banded stack of bills in hand. He recoiled, his eyes fixed on the gun pointed at his chest.

Feeling dizzy, Jenny retreated a half-step and adjusted her grip.

"Thought you could cheat me, huh? Put the money on the desk. Then lie face down on the floor, spread your legs, and put your hands behind your head."

He held one hand to the side, extended the cash with the other.

"Don't do anything stupid, Jenny. Take the money and split."

That's what her man wanted them to do. "We'll make a run for it," he'd said, "someplace far from L.A. where Freddy can't find us."

But she wasn't leaving town. Why give up her Hollywood dream, just when it felt so close?

The gun wobbled despite tightening her grip.

She raised her voice. "On the floor. Now."

He showed her his palms. "Okay, okay. You can have it all."

He turned to face the desk, then pivoted, swinging the briefcase in a wide arc and knocking the gun across the room.

She froze, then fumbled in her pocket. As she drew out her hand, his fist exploded against her temple.

Falling against the door, she dropped in a heap. Her can of pepper spray clattered across the floor while the room spun and her ears rang.

She felt his hands grip her calves. He jerked her toward him, her head hitting the floor with a thud.

A knee crushed her chest. A foot pinned her arm. His thick fingers dug into her neck as his thumbs pressed against her throat.

Searing pain, like a bone breaking.

Gasping, she tried to pry off his fingers with her free hand, but no use. She jabbed her nails at his face, but he moved his head out of reach.

Her arm crashed to the floor. Her legs flailed. A shoe came off. Then the other.

The room disappeared, then returned.

Above her, his tar-stained teeth froze in a grimace. His face blurred.

Darkness again.

Her body shuddered then went still.

The refrigerator hum faded away.

Rollins dragged Jenny's body into the bathroom. He collected her gun, pepper spray, purse, and shoes, tossed them inside the bathroom, and closed the door.

Wiping sweat from his face with his sleeve, he grabbed his cell and dialed a number. On hearing Eugene's voice, he exhaled hard.

"Eugene. Where are you?"

"I'm in Venice for the last two guys."

"I need you back at the trailer. Now." He chewed his lip. "Jenny had an accident."

"You call nine-one-one?"

"Fuck, no. You still got tarps and shovels in your trunk?"

A long moment of silence. "Yeah. I got 'em."

"Good. Get over here now."

He ended the call and checked his watch. It would take Eugene at least twenty minutes to get to the trailer. Grabbing a flashlight, he headed to the backyard.

In the end, the senator had caved to his asking price—a hundred and fifty grand—more money than he'd ever had at one time. He planned to leave it buried behind the trailer while he figured out how to launder it.

Though he'd been sure no one had seen him hide the money, Jenny's quip about being cheated made him suspicious.

He shined the flashlight around the yard. A tall, tarp-covered fence separated the trailer park from a housing project at the back. Little risk of being seen from that end. Ditto for the vacant unit on the right. And no signs of life from the drunk's trailer to his left.

He grabbed the shovel from the bushes where he'd hidden it. Hurrying to the boulder, he shut off the lamp to let his eyes adjust to the moonlight.

Crouching, he pushed against the stone. It budged a bit, but the ground beneath had sunk, forming a crater.

Using the shovel, he scraped dirt from around the boulder. He gave it another heave, moving it several inches, all that he'd need. He dug a hole and shoved his hand inside.

Nothing there.

He sat on the ground and pushed the stone with his feet—grunting so loud he checked to make sure he hadn't roused the neighbor. The boulder budged a few more inches. He dug a wider, deeper hole.

Falling to his knees, he clawed at the dirt like a wild animal. But no money bags.

He cursed under his breath and fired the shovel across the yard. It clanged against the fence and thudded to the ground.

Sitting on his haunches, he looked around with wide eyes. Had the senator's guys followed him to the trailer? Other than them, only Jenny knew he'd gotten a payoff that afternoon. But she couldn't have moved that stone.

Not alone, anyway.

He turned his head slowly toward his bathroom window where a night light gave off a faint glow. He raced inside and examined Jenny's hands. Dirt below the nails, and two of her fake nails missing.

Shaking her by the shoulders, he screamed into her face. "Where'd you put it, you stupid bitch?"

Her head hung back, exposing the deep bruises on her neck. He dropped her onto the floor and covered his mouth with his fist.

Fuck! How would he find the money now?

He dumped the contents of her purse and looked inside the zipper compartments. Only chick's shit—no cash.

He took a deep breath, trying to cool down and think. Find the guy who helped her with the stone, and he would find his money.

Grabbing her phone, he checked the text log.

He moaned. "No. No way."

Loud knocks rocked the trailer's front door.

Adrenaline shot Rollins to his feet. "Eugene?"

"Open up. Police!" A second later, the door burst open and four uniformed cops stormed in, guns drawn. They grabbed and cuffed him and threw him on his knees.

Rollins shook his head, teeth bared in a sneer. "Fucking Eugene."

Two black-and-whites and an ambulance crowded the street in front of the trailer. Eugene watched the action from his parked car a half-block away. The quick police response had surprised him. They must've arrived within minutes of his 9-1-1 call.

He twirled the diamond ring on his pinky finger, the one he got off a doper in lieu of cash. His chest felt heavy, like that boulder was sitting on top.

He'd never been so sad. Not for Freddy, who would get what he deserved. But for Jenny, stupid girl. Nothing was ever enough for her—least of all, him.

Hadn't he warned her not to go back to the trailer, and pleaded with her to leave town? But Jenny wouldn't give up Hollywood—and Freddy stood in the way.

Putting the city lights in his rearview, he drove east out of town until the desert crept up to the road. He pulled off at a gas station next to nowhere, Nevada. An attendant sat behind the cashier's cage, head buried in his phone.

Eugene parked behind the station, got out, and opened his trunk. The wind whipped his pantlegs with a sound like laundry shook out to dry.

He unzipped two matching duffels, his and Jenny's, which he'd packed with some clothes and the cash. Between the money pit and the dopers, they'd scored a hundred and eighty grand.

He'd split it into two bags of ninety thousand dollars, putting one in each case. Letting out a long exhale, he moved Jenny's cash to his duffel.

He took out her blue silk blouse—the one that matched her eyes. Rubbing it against his cheek, he inhaled her scent.

A sigh lifted and dropped his shoulders. Jenny would've looked good on his arm at the Four Seasons in Vegas.

After dumping the rest of her things in a trash bin, he went to the open field behind the station. Around him, nothing but wind and tumbleweed, and a starry desert sky.

Letting a gust lift the blouse, he watched it flutter into the night, like a lonely bluebird winging toward the stars.

GHOSTS OF CHARACTERS PAST

Kathy Krevat

Someone sat on my bed, humming.

That wouldn't be so surprising except that I had a single room at the lodge. With a lock. My heart raced.

"I know you're awake." A woman's voice sounded amused. "You stopped snoring."

I peeked through a crack in my eyelids. The sheer curtains let in enough light for me to see a short woman with red hair perched at the foot of my bed. I sat up and slid as far away from her as I could, knocking my spine against the wooden headboard. "Who?" My voice cracked. I cleared my throat. "Who are you? What are you doing here?" I'd met the other guests for the writers' retreat the evening before. She wasn't one of them.

"Really?" She scowled. "You don't recognize me? Maybe it's because you changed the color of my eyes from hazel to cocoa brown in the last revision."

"Wha—?" My lips refused to work correctly. "Kendra?"

"Bingo!" She jumped off the bed and her feet hit the floor with a loud thump. "Now get up. You have work to do."

I brought my knees to my chest and closed my eyes. "I'm hallucinating."

"Nope," she assured me. "I'm really here. I even made Sea Salt Caramel Cupcakes while all of you writers slept."

The scent of something delicious registered. "But you're..." I started.

She put her fists on her hips. "A fictional character you wrote for your mystery series and then *abandoned* when your contract didn't get extended?"

"Uh..." I shook my head. That was impossible.

"Today is the day you, bestselling author Winnie Dalton, are going to change all that." She raised her chin, a challenging glint in her eyes.

"What?"

"All you have to do to save me from that hellhole of nothingness is to write me into your next book." She spoke as if she'd figured out everything. "Surely San Diego can use an expert baker-slash-mystery-solving genius."

"I can't," I objected. "It's in my contract. I'm not allowed to use you again."

"You can just change my name! I always wanted to be a Madison."

"Maybe." I trailed off as my traitorous brain was already figuring out how to slide her in. "But I already have a character with a name that starts with M."

"Okay, let's go with Rochelle." She got louder.

"You'll have to wait for book two." I started off strong, but she narrowed her eyes and I weakly added, "Book one's already in editing."

"Oh please." She waved her hand. "You always make a ton of changes in the first edit. And the second, if I remember correctly."

"I'm not supposed to," I said. "I'm working on fixing that. It drives my copy editor crazy."

"Are you also 'fixing' your problem with deadlines?" She used finger quotes, sounding like a smart-alecky teen.

I shook my head, not as an answer to her question, but because this whole situation was insane.

She threw herself into the desk chair and wheeled it across

the hardwood floor. "It's totally boring in East Charles now that we're stuck there with no mysteries," she whined. "At least there's some excitement in your zombie book."

"You read my zombie manuscript?" My voice squeaked. I wasn't showing that to anyone. Especially not my agent. She hated horror.

"I live in your computer," Kendra said. "I visit other stories to keep my sanity. It was either the zombie book or that ridiculous *Mad Men* fan fiction."

"Shhh!" I glared at her, embarrassed to my core.

"You need more guts." She pointed her finger at me. "In the zombie book. Not like courage guts. Guts-guts."

"Now you're a critic?" I stood up. How could I be arguing with a fictional character?

"No, now I'm an Amazon reviewer," she said. "We're ruthless. So you better make me awesome in your new series, or I'll go all one-star-savage on you."

I stared at her, blinking.

She smiled as if she'd won. "Let's talk about Rochelle."

It was time to squash this whole idea. "I already have an R character, too!"

Kendra crossed her arms. "You should start listening to those readers who say they can't keep track of your characters. You have too many." She made an elaborate shrug.

"Why did you shrug?" I asked.

She smirked. "Overusing 'shrug' is another one of your problems."

I closed my eyes and plopped back down on the bed. "You are a hallucination."

"If I was a hallucination, then no one else could see me, right?"

I opened my eyes. "Right."

Kendra disappeared, and before I could feel relieved, I heard a scream from the next room. She was back in a flash. "See? Not a hallucination."

I scowled and then stomped out into the hall to the next

room. I knocked. "Are you okay?"

A woman opened the door a crack, wearing a confused expression and pajamas plastered with rainbow unicorns. "I thought I saw a woman sitting on the dresser, but then she was gone."

"Huh." I tried to reassure her. "Maybe it was a trick of the light or something?"

"I guess." She looked around cautiously, as if afraid Kendra would pop out again. "I wish I had my sage here so I could smudge this place."

When I got back to my room, Kendra was gone, and I felt oddly disappointed. Yesterday, I'd been delighted to escape the noise and traffic of downtown San Diego and head northeast for my annual writers' retreat in Julian—home of bulging apple pies, gold-panning, and historic buildings from the earliest days of the Gold Rush. Fall in Julian was gorgeous, with crisp mornings and leaves changing to vibrant colors. And did I mention apple pies?

I sat down on the bed just as my cell phone started playing *It's Raining Men*, the ring tone of my next-door neighbor, Peggy.

"Winnie? Are you home?" Her tone was urgent.

"No," I said. "I told you that I'm in Julian this weekend."

"Oh no." She sounded scared.

"What?"

"I heard someone in your apartment last night, and I figured it was you, that you decided not to go."

"Shit." We always complained about how thin the walls were in the building, but now it was a bonus. Anxiety pushed against my chest. "Did you check?"

"I'm standing in front of your apartment now," she said. "Your door is open a little bit."

"Oh my god." My heart pounded. "Can you peek in and see if anything is missing?"

"Okay, hold on." She gasped. "It's been ransacked!"

***

Since I'd barely unpacked, I was out the door and driving down the mountain in a few minutes. I stopped at the end of the long driveway that led from the lodge to the highway and belatedly pulled out my phone to find the fastest way home.

When I looked to my right to make sure it was safe to pull out, Kendra was sitting in the passenger seat. I jumped and swore.

"Why don't you put those words in your books?" She buckled her seatbelt.

"I write cozies." I took a few deep breaths to calm myself down. "My characters don't curse. And what are you trying to do? Give me a heart attack?"

"Of course not." She pursed her lips. "I'm still getting the hang of traveling back and forth."

"Where did you go?" I asked.

"I thought I was going back to your apartment," she explained. "I can move between your laptop and your desktop computer but not too far beyond either."

"Okay." How much weirder could this situation get?

"But I wasn't at your apartment." She sounded perplexed. "I was in the back seat of a—Watch out!"

A pickup truck with a huge metal grill crashed into us, and everything went black.

I came to with an airbag in my face and steam pouring out from under the hood of the car. Kendra was shaking me. "Wake up," she yelled.

"Don't move her," an unfamiliar voice said. "She could have a concussion or internal injuries."

A woman with long blond hair stood outside the car, peering at me over librarian glasses. She was holding my phone.

I blinked with disbelief. "Hope?"

She smiled, showing the space between her front teeth. "You recognized me!"

"You sound different than I expected," I said.

"If you weren't specific in your descriptions, we filled in the rest." She spoke in the clear tone of a teacher, watching my face. "What do you think of my voice?"

"It's lovely." I realized she was subtly trying to assess if my brain was working. "Can I get out of here?"

"First, how does your head feel?" Hope asked.

"Fine," I insisted, feeling claustrophobic. "Just get me out."

She pointed to the truck-sized dent in my door. "I don't think this one will work."

"Whoa." I could've easily been killed. My car was off the road, tilting sideways into a ditch.

"The engine is starting to smoke," Kendra warned. "It could catch on fire." From the passenger seat, she pushed the airbags aside and unbuckled both seatbelts. She helped me maneuver out on her side.

I stood up and wobbled.

"Take it easy." Kendra steadied me.

"You're not hurt?" I asked.

"Must be part of the whole deal." She flashed me a wry grin. "Being fictional and all."

The three of us walked away from the car and Hope made me sit down on a boulder. She frowned into my phone. "The ambulance should be here soon."

"Who did this?" I asked.

"You should stay quiet," Hope said.

Kendra ignored her. "This truck looked like it was about to turn into the driveway to the lodge, but then the driver aimed right for us. He pushed us off the road, then backed up and got out of his truck. He was like a giant, like, way over six feet tall and he wore mirrored sunglasses, like the Terminator! No, like the villain in your first book! He reached in through the broken window and grabbed your backpack."

"My new laptop?" I put my head in my hands. "This doesn't make any sense."

"Sounds like we have a mystery to solve." They sat down on either side of me.

"Wait." I turned toward Hope. "What are you doing here?"

"My original plan was to help with the Character Protection Plan, but I arrived just in time for this." She gestured toward the crushed car.

"What plan?" I was so confused that I thought I might really have a concussion.

"Like you humans have the Witness Protection Plan," she explained. "You'll give us new identities in your next book. We'll keep a low profile and no one will ever know."

"My new publisher—" I began.

"Will be none the wiser." Hope sounded sure of herself.

"I'm not changing my book at this stage, because you two are bored back in—" I hesitated.

"East Charles." Hope gently reminded me of the town's name in the series.

"I know East Charles," I said. "I meant Fictionland. Or wherever you guys are from."

Kendra and Hope exchanged a look.

"What does that mean?" I asked.

They both shrugged.

"And stop shrugging!" I took a few deep breaths.

Hope put her hand on my shoulder. "Let's focus on the man who stole your laptop."

Kendra crossed her legs. "Before I was so rudely interrupted by that lunatic, I was telling Winnie that I saw her home computer in the back seat of a black pickup truck. It can't be a coincidence that a black truck ran us off the road." She paused. "Wait. Why are we both here? There's no computer."

I pulled out my sunflower necklace from inside the collar of my shirt. "Maybe because of this? It's a thumb drive. I make backups every night."

"How would someone know where to find you?" Hope asked.

"I have a calendar on my fridge," I guessed. "If this pickup truck guy ransacked my apartment, he could have seen where I was."

"What?" Kendra said. "Your apartment was ransacked?"

A wave of exhaustion rushed over me as a siren sounded in the distance. I shook my head. "What is happening?"

Kendra clapped her hands. "We're having an adventure."

"I don't have adventures." My voice rose to a wail. "I write about them."

Hope tilted her head. "Looks like you're having one now."

The ambulance rounded the corner, and they both disappeared.

The closest emergency room was in Escondido, and I wasn't released until after Detective Robin Sanchez grilled me about the burglary in my house. She'd found a listening device planted in my dining room and suspected there might be more.

That news had put me over the edge, and I'd sobbed through the few details I could dredge up about the accident. Unfortunately, I wasn't able to give her anything helpful, like a license plate. She didn't seem to believe my theory that it could be related to my latest book, but dutifully took down names of people I'd recently talked to for research.

The detective left my emergency room cubicle and then returned. "Who called nine-one-one?"

"Beats me." I couldn't mention Kendra or Hope without sounding like I had a major head injury.

It was only early afternoon, and I was already exhausted. Peggy picked me up and drove me to the closest Rent-A-Wreck.

She frowned at the ramshackle building surrounded by cars whose best days were behind them. "I wish 'bestselling author' meant what I thought it meant before you told me the deep dark secrets of the publishing industry."

I wasn't too tired to laugh. "Thanks for the ride."

She pushed aside a strand of curly black hair from her face

and gave me her "mom" look. "I think we should talk about why someone broke into your apartment and then crashed into you and stole your laptop. It's like a plot from one of your books."

Her worry made the fear rush in, and I had to blink back tears. "I've been trying not to think about it. Maybe it has something to do with my new series. But that's crazy." *As crazy as my characters coming to life?*

"The one with the low-income housing developer victim and the politician suspect?" Peggy loved to brainstorm stories with me and was an expert at finding plot holes. "Did you tell Detective Sanchez that?"

I nodded. "She's going to talk to everyone I interviewed for research." I patted my pants pocket to make sure her business card was there, like a talisman against anything else bad happening to me.

"You can stay with me," she offered.

"I should stay away from my apartment for a few days, and you're right next door." Plus, maybe it wasn't safe for her to be around me. I used the door handle to stand up, my body aching in places it had never ached before. "Thanks for the ride."

Once I chose my car—a dark gray 2006 Honda Civic—and signed the paperwork, I drove a few blocks away and pulled over. I took out my phone and brought up the list of people I'd recently interviewed for my book: a housing developer who had weirdly claimed at the end of the interview that most of his rivals worked with the Russian mob, an elementary school teacher who used to be in foster care, and a stripper who also worked as a coffee barista. None of them looked like Kendra's description of the guy in mirrored sunglasses. Sometimes my plots got a little far-fetched, but imagining any of these people being involved with the Terminator Man was too much, even for me.

For a minute, I missed Kendra and Hope. Maybe they really could help. Of course, I'd written them to be great mystery solvers.

My first step was to replace my laptop. I drove to Junior's Pawn Shop, where my friend George worked with his dad. He'd given me a great deal on my last laptop, and I'd have to hit him up for the friends and family discount again.

When I arrived, yellow crime scene tape surrounded the small store at the end of an aging strip mall.

Anxiety ran up my spine as I parked. I asked the first police officer I saw, "What happened?"

"Double homicide." He held his hand up. "Stay back."

Oh no!

I joined the crowd gathered behind the tape. Crime scene investigators were combing through everything inside the store.

"I heard that they tortured the dad." An older man in a Padres hat sounded worried.

The blood rushed from my head, and I sat down hard on the curb. After a few deep breaths, the little birds floating around my head stopped chirping, and I called Peggy. She answered immediately. I went hoarse with fear. "Don't go home."

I turned off my phone and drove like a CIA operative, doubling back and making U-turns until I was sure no one was following me. I stopped at a hole-in-the-wall burger place and chose a stool at the counter where I could see outside. No one seemed interested in me or my car.

Taking a deep breath, I turned my phone on just long enough to download a map and then I put it in airplane mode, hoping no one could track me. I drove through an ATM to take out cash, stopped at a used computer store to buy the cheapest laptop I could find, and then followed my GPS instructions to a motel I'd researched for a previous book. They took cash and had discreet parking spots behind the building.

The room on the second floor smelled like body odor and rotten food. The comforter was threadbare, and one end of the closet door was dangling from the track. My body aches had intensified, and I lifted my shirt in front of the mirror. Vicious bruises bloomed along my side and shoulder.

I placed the laptop on the tiny, scarred desk and balanced on a chair with a loose wheel. When I uploaded the files from my thumb drive, Kendra and Hope appeared at my shoulders. The relief I felt was overwhelming.

"Oh good," Kendra said. "You're checking your files. We were thinking the same thing. Isn't that weird?"

"Well, you are the product of my imagination," I told her, keeping my eyes on the file names scrolling up the screen.

"And your intelligence," Hope added.

Kendra held her nose. "Why does it stink in here?" She added, "And thanks so much for giving me excellent smelling as a character trait." Her sarcasm was apparent even with the clenched nose.

"It's certainly an asset for a baker," Hope reminded her.

"Okay. This might be the problem." I pointed to a bunch of Excel files downloading from my thumb drive onto the laptop, each labeled with a month, year, and followed by "Receipts."

Hope leaned closer to the computer. "I'm assuming those aren't your documents."

I shook my head and opened one.

The number of zeroes at the bottom of the columns made Kendra whistle. "That looks like a lot of motive."

Hope took the laptop from me to analyze the spreadsheets.

"I can't believe this," I groaned. "George and his dad are dead!"

Kendra paced the small room. "That is concerning."

"Concerning?" I asked.

She paused. "You're the one who made me cool under pressure." She stopped behind Hope. "Anything?"

"I'm guessing they're loan payments," she answered. "The interest rates are excessive, so perhaps you somehow got a loan shark's computer."

"Oh great." I felt light-headed again but afraid to lie down on the bed. "The freakin' mob is after me."

"You look pale," Hope said gently. "Put your head between your knees."

Unfortunately, that brought me closer to the carpet with ground-in stains that I didn't want to think about and the smell of rotting fruit. I sat back up and held my nose like Kendra.

Hope continued. "These files have a lot of details."

I pulled the comforter off the bed and threw it to the floor, before sitting on the bed beside her. "What do you mean?"

"If I click on the dollar amounts, it takes me to account information with names and addresses."

"So we have, like, real evidence of crimes from a freakin' loan shark with his victims' names and everything?" My voice rose an octave. "I'm calling the detective."

They looked at each other.

"What?" I demanded.

"I guess those who can't do, write about it." Kendra scowled. "Where's your sense of adventure?"

"It's in my books," I said, insulted. "Do you know what a risk it is to put everything into a project and let it out into the world?"

"That is difficult." Hope nodded with exaggerated sympathy.

Kendra looked away.

Oh man. I felt like a mother who had disappointed her children.

"Okay, what's your idea?" I asked. "But I'm telling you right now, I'm not going to be one of those too-stupid-to-live characters."

We compromised. First, I called Detective Sanchez, who was happy to come to my room and pick up the evidence. "Email it to me immediately," she demanded.

She was less happy about the idea for luring Terminator Man into the open but agreed to bring backup for the stakeout.

Next, I called Peggy's home number and left a loud message, hoping that any listening devices in my apartment would pick it up through the thin walls. "Peggy, this is Winnie. I found some weird files on my computer that I think are the problem. I'm going to give them to the police. I think that'll fix everything. Oh, and if you're looking for me, I'm at the Southwest Inn, not too far away." I hung up and turned to Kendra and Hope. "I hope you're right, that catching this guy red-handed is the best solution."

"Don't you want to get out of this place?" Kendra asked.

Hope added, "This way, we'll get our man faster and you won't have to be looking over your shoulder."

I moved to the window to watch for the detective. The parking lot looked like something out of an old-timey movie, with an over-flowing dumpster and oily puddles of water reflecting the flashing orange and blue motel sign.

I closed my eyes for a moment and took a few deep breaths, trying to relax. When I opened them, a black pickup truck with a dented front grill was pulling into the parking lot. "Oh my God, he's here." That grill probably still had pieces of my door on it.

The truck pulled into a spot by the office, and the maybe-too-aptly-named Terminator Man stepped out.

Kendra joined me at the window. "How did he get here so fast?"

"I don't know," I wailed. "Maybe he found this place in my research." I looked toward the street. "Where's the detective?"

"Call her again," Hope suggested.

I followed her advice, keeping my eyes on the scary dude. He headed toward the front office.

"Shit," I said just as the detective answered.

"Who is this?" she demanded.

"It's Winnie." My voice trembled. "When are you getting

here? That man that, I mean, who ran me off the road just arrived."

"Hold on," she tried to assure me. "I'll be there in a few minutes."

She turned her siren on, and I hung up.

We peered out the window again.

Terminator Man stood in the center of the parking lot, staring right at us.

We all jumped back, making the blinds flutter.

"Stall him!" Hope called out, as they slid into the closet.

In what seemed like seconds, he was pounding on the door, shaking it in its frame.

My breath whistled out. "Who is it?"

He didn't answer, just turned the knob hard and pushed. He put some weight into the next shove and the door gave way, soon followed by the chain popping out of the wall.

He stepped inside. "Give me the files."

"What files?" I squeaked.

He grabbed my arm and twisted it up behind my back. "Give me the files now."

"What are you talking about?" I gasped, my arm screaming with pain.

He yanked harder. "We know you copied the files. I want those copies. All of them."

Tears filled my eyes, and I pointed to the thumb drive on the desk. "Those files?"

He let go, and I landed awkwardly on the bed.

I held my arm against my chest, rubbing my abused shoulder. "I don't understand." My whole body shook. "What's so important about them?"

He picked up the thumb drive, giving a slight shake of his head at the sunflower cover as if angry at himself for missing it. He tucked it into his shirt pocket and pulled out a gun from the back of his waistband. It had a silencer on it.

"What? Why do you have to do that?" I held my arms out like

that would help me. "I don't know anything about anything!"

"You're a loose end." His voice was cold.

"Don't shoot!" I yelled as Kendra and Hope slammed open the sliding door. It promptly came off of its track, falling and hitting the back of Terminator Man's knees. He fell clumsily, shooting on the way down, the bullet hitting the wall right beside me.

Kendra and Hope both jumped on his back, but he kept the gun in his hand, attempting to aim at any and all of us.

I picked up the piece-of-crap chair and slammed it down on his wrist with a satisfying crunch. At last, he dropped the gun.

"Freeze!" I heard from behind me.

I'd never been so happy to see the police before in my life.

Detective Sanchez stopped by the next day as I was cleaning up my apartment with Peggy's help. She told me that a bunch of computers had been stolen from one of those shady quick-loan businesses and pawned at George's shop. I'd been the unlucky recipient of one of them. Unfortunately for me, mine held unencrypted documents tracking the firm's most risky loans. The business was already under investigation for knowingly approving loans based on stolen identities. The manager had panicked and hired Terrence Wilson, aka Terminator Man, to do whatever was necessary to get the files back. He'd taken the manager at his word, torturing George and his dad to find out who bought the computers, and then coming after me.

As thanks to Kendra and Hope for saving my life, I put them in the book. Hope was now Willow, the town librarian, and Kendra was Yolanda, the homeschooling mom who won all the local baking competitions.

They appeared later in the day while I was putting the finishing touches on the character changes.

"Thank you." Hope gave my arm a squeeze. "We are going to have so much fun!" She disappeared.

"Wait," I protested. "She means in the book, right?"

"And remember, my eyes are now brown, not hazel." Kendra smiled. She hugged me, holding me tight. "I'll see you soon," she whispered, her voice full of emotion.

Tears spilled out of my eyes, and I wiped them away. "Not too soon, I hope."

She shrugged, winked, and disappeared.

FOURTEEN YEARS

Axel Milens

I was returning home from walking my dog, Barbie Number 3, when I noticed the neighbor's fence being painted. I adjusted my sweater vest, which has a propensity to bunch up above my stomach, and, peering above my bifocals, asked the painter if he'd be available to do my fence later.

Not because it needed it—the redwood is riddled with termite holes and should be replaced—but because, other than my dog, I hadn't talked to anyone in more than ten days and I felt the need for some human interaction.

The painter, a man in his late thirties with slicked-back hair, turned his sweaty face toward me. He wore faded jeans and soiled sneakers. Holding his paint roller in midair, he jerked his chin. "How much you pay?"

A fat gold chain wriggled over the collar of his paint-stained T-shirt. Because of his accent, I pinged him as Eastern European. Barbie Number 3 let out a tired yap. I asked how much he wanted.

"Hundred bucks."

"Twenty-five," I said.

"Fifty. No prep." He pronounced 'prep' with an upbeat intonation, rolling the R as if he'd just learned the word and was showing off his newly acquired proficiency in the language. I agreed, but not before making sure the paint would be included.

He said he had an old can of yellow in his truck.

It was one of those Southern California spring afternoons, when the sunshine gently warms your skin, the air smells fresh and it feels good to be outside. Having absolutely nothing else to do, I watched the painter—he'd introduced himself as Tibor—impatiently slap the roller on the grayish wood separating my dried-up lawn from the street.

After a while, I wondered what I had gotten myself into. Not only was the color too bright for my weathered house, but Tibor was a slob.

"Why don't you protect the pavement with plastic or something?" I leaned on my rusty mailbox. "The paint is dripping all over the place."

Tibor frowned. "Paint dripping normal," he barked. "Paint always dripping."

"How are you going to clean it off the concrete?"

"I remove. No problem."

Tibor wasn't going to get his fifty dollars until that pavement was spotless. "It would be easier to cover it before the paint falls on it," I said. "And a lot less work."

He hit the wood hard with the engorged paint roller, splattering yellow on his T-shirt. "No problem," he shouted. "I already say, I remove later." With his right foot, he crushed a little snail crawling on the dirt at the bottom of the fence.

"Why in the hell did you do that?" I choked on my words.

He stayed silent, teeth clenched, and kept painting.

I shook my head and watched him for a while. There were faded tattoos in Cyrillic on both his forearms. I wondered what this brute's story was, if he was connected to a nefarious criminal underworld of one kind or another. Then, it hit me: could he be the man I'd been looking for? The man I needed to finally execute the plan I'd been mulling over for the last fourteen years?

"Tibor." My voice shook. "I apologize in advance for what I'm about to ask. If you feel my question is insulting in any way, please ignore it."

He frowned and looked at me. "What?"

I cleared my throat, adjusted my glasses. "Would you happen to know, by chance, anyone who can"—I ran my index finger across my throat—"someone?"

Not that I thought FBI agents were hiding in the bushes, lip-reading our conversation with binoculars, but I was paranoid. I'd read news stories about people convicted for just talking about this sort of thing.

Tibor dipped the roller and continued to paint. He stared at the fence with a tense face while my legs grew weak from nerves. Then he growled, "I do it."

My heart jumped. "You? Are you sure?"

"I am professional."

Not as a painter, I scoffed silently. But it was fair to assume taking someone's life required a different set of skills. Was this guy the real thing, or planning to swindle an old man? I thought it over for a few minutes, then I pushed my concerns aside. I had no choice. It had been fourteen years and I hadn't done a thing. I was turning seventy in two weeks. I couldn't really trust that goon, but this was my last chance. If I went along with him, monitored his every move, paid him only after the job was done, that could work. I felt energized by my decision.

"How much?"

He didn't look at me. "Ten thousand."

"Are you serious? Come on, that's too much." I pointed at the peeling clapboard of my old house. "I'm on Social Security."

He shrugged.

"It will be a cakewalk," I added. "The man is seventy-six."

After dropping the roller in the can, Tibor placed his fists on his hips and faced me. "Okay, for old man, discount. Eight thousand."

"Eight grand? For crying out loud, at his age, the man is basically already dead. I should pay half price, at the most."

Tibor grunted then lifted his eyes to the sky. "You, stingy man. Best price: five thousand. Take it or leave it."

"Fine," I said. I would have to survive on canned sardines for a while, but it was worth it.

He extended his right hand. "Business deal. Shake."

I pulled my hand behind my back. "Can't you see you have paint all over your fingers? Let's talk about the plan."

A week later, Tibor and I sat in my Ford Escort. To make sure he'd show up, I had only given him a two-hundred-dollar advance. We were in Sherman Oaks above Ventura Boulevard, parked under the shade of mature elm trees. Across the wide avenue stood Charlie Kolshak's two-story house, the kind with a glossy green lawn and a white picket fence intertwined with blooming jasmine bushes.

Tibor, dressed for the part in a black hoodie, black sweatpants, and brand-new white sneakers, clutched a baseball bat between his legs. I could feel heat emanating from his body while he squirmed continuously in the seat. The sour smell of his sweat filled the car.

"Relax," I said, cracking the window. "You've done this before, right?"

"How you know old man is coming now?" he mumbled.

"Kolshak is like a train, always on time. At 3 p.m., he'll come through that front door." I had spent enough hours sitting in my car, spying on him with binoculars, to know his schedule by heart.

Tibor wiped his wet brow with the back of his hand. "Why you want old man dead?"

"He stole my wife," I barked, annoyed at the questioning. I wasn't going to share my life's story and tell him that fourteen years ago, I'd come home unexpectedly to find Barbie, my wife, and Charlie Kolshak—at the time my best friend and business partner—going at it on the living room carpet. I had tried to forgive Barbie. The kids, both in college at the time, had pushed us hard to reconcile, but what did they know? Finally, after the divorce, Barbie had moved in with Kolshak. I had never forgotten and never forgiven.

"How old, your wife?"

"She was fifty-five at the time."

Tibor tilted his head back and let loose a deep, throaty laugh, revealing stained yellowish teeth. "Who cares about old lady wife? Good opportunity to get rid of her. You get a new one. Young one. Nice tits and ass. Not saggy."

The blood rose to my face. "That's not how it works, Tibor. Have you ever been in love? Do you even know what love is?"

Tibor laughed again. "Love is for stupid people. Tibor no love. Sex only."

I felt a violent revulsion toward the lout, one nearly as strong as my hate for Kolshak. I wasn't sure how the conversation would have ended, but at that moment, Kolshak came out of his house. A dried-up little man in beige pants, wearing a green visor and tottering under the weight of a large golf bag full of clubs. He walked toward the silver Mercedes parked in his driveway.

"Time to do your job," I said. Tibor's face collapsed in a sudden bout of anxiety. I was sure by now he'd never done such a thing, but it was too late to retreat. "Remember, it has to look like a mugging gone wrong in case there is a witness. You ask for his wallet, and when he refuses—I know the man, he will—you knock him on the head with the bat."

Tibor let out a long sigh and pulled his hood over his head. "Okay, I go."

The car door slammed, and I watched him cross the street, head down, the bat half-hidden inside his jacket. My heart was beating so hard my chest hurt.

Kolshak was placing the golf bag into his open trunk when Tibor confronted him. There was a brief exchange of words, then Kolshak lifted a palm and reached for the back of his pants. Okay, I was wrong about the wallet. That shouldn't have mattered, but Tibor stood there, waiting. "Go for it!" I screamed inside the car, about to pass out from anxiety. Suddenly fearful I could be heard, I said, under my breath, "Stealing his wallet is not the point, you idiot."

The rest happened fast. Kolshak extended his arm and sprayed something in Tibor's face. Tibor dropped the bat and, folding in half, brought his hands to his eyes. Kolshak extracted a golf club out of the bag in a swift, graceful move and took a swing, hitting Tibor on the side of the head. By the time that dolt collapsed onto the driveway, I was already rummaging in the glove compartment, my cheeks on fire.

"I knew it, I knew it, I knew it," I mumbled to myself, visualizing the yellow paint splashed all over the pavement. "That's what I get for hiring a goddamn klutz off the street."

I grabbed my 25-caliber pistol, which I've owned since carjacking was all the rage in L.A. in the eighties, and tried to get out of the car.

The buckled seat belt held me back. I fumbled to unbuckle it, my glasses getting foggy from my panicked breathing. Finally, I extricated myself, but not before banging my head on the door jamb. Out of breath, my left temple pulsating with pain, I shuffled across the street as fast as I could, gun in hand.

"Kolshak," I tried to scream, my voice sounding like gurgled bleating.

Talking on his cell phone, he glared at me from behind his thick glasses. I was a few feet away when he opened his mouth wide and dropped his arm. "Neufeld! What in the world? Boy, am I glad to see you!"

I was going to do it, I swear, but the beaming smile on his wrinkled face stopped me cold. With his cell phone, he pointed at Tibor on the ground. "Look what happened. I just got mugged. In the Valley, in the middle of the day, can you believe it?" His smile faded. "But how did... What are you doing here and what's with the gun?"

"I was passing by," I muttered. "I saw it happen and pulled over to help."

"Talk about a coincidence," Kolshak said with a chuckle. His smile beamed brighter and he opened his arms wide. "Come here, you schmuck! How many years has it been? So wonderful to see you."

And there we stood, hugging each other tight and patting each other's backs, him holding his phone, me the gun, as if there had never been any falling out between us.

We parted. Kolshak put a hand on my shoulder and stared at me, his eyes misty behind his Coke-bottle lenses. "I miss her every day." His voice broke and he gulped. "Every day."

Six years ago, Barbie had died of breast cancer.

"Me too." As I said the words, the image of Barbie stealthily walking around the house in high heels, fly swatter in hand, exclaiming, "Aha, got you sucker!" every time she killed a fly absurdly came into my mind. My heart filled with sorrow.

Kolshak squeezed my shoulder. "She suffered a lot, but she was brave until the end."

I nodded.

"She asked for you. She wanted to know if you'd forgiven her." He paused. "But you never came." There was both reproach and a tender understanding in his tone.

The kids had begged me to go and say goodbye, but I hadn't listened. I missed her. But I also hated her for cheating on me, for destroying my friendship with Kolshak, for forcing us to split the business, and for me ending up in a one-room office above a mini mart on Pico, while Kolshak, who'd been followed by most of the clientele, moved into a luxurious suite on the fifteenth floor of a Century City office tower. I hated her for proving, in the end, that he was a bigger man than I was.

"I couldn't..." I lowered my eyes, unable to continue. What was the point of making excuses? I had none.

"That's all right." He switched to a lighter tone. "All in the past. No point dwelling on it. We'd better make the most of the time we've got left, right? Do you play golf? I hit the links with the fellows twice a week at Balboa. You wanna join us?"

He let go of my shoulder and tears came to my eyes. It had been fourteen years since I'd experienced the touch of another human being. There was a warmth in my chest I hadn't felt for a very long time. I glimpsed something bright, as if decade-old clouds were lifting to reveal a bright blue sky I had been unable to see for all these years.

Maybe this was what forgiveness felt like.

Kolshak looked at me with an affectionate smile. "What do you say, Neufeld? It'll be fun."

"I'd love to."

There was a flash of motion, then a loud crack.

Kolshak crumbled in a heap at my feet. I opened my mouth to scream but no sound came out. Tibor stood next to me, red-rimmed eyes, sticky blood smeared on the side of his face, bat in hand. I felt dizzy. Everything churned inside me. Before I could do anything, Tibor whacked poor Kolshak on the head a second time. This time, the cracking sound was even louder.

"Little problem to start, but job finished now. Old man dead." Tibor looked at me, grinning and nodding, as if expecting a compliment.

My entire body shook. My eyes went from Tibor's smirking mug to Kolshak's face, turned up to the sky, his green visor askew. A dark bruise was forming on his forehead. His eyes were closed, as if he were asleep. There was a peaceful smile on his lips.

"My best friend," I cried. "You killed him!"

I lifted the gun and shot Tibor in the face. The bullet shattered his front teeth, and a flying shard of enamel tore my right cheek. He looked baffled for a second then collapsed against the trunk of the Mercedes with a thud before tumbling down to the ground. The bat rolled down the slope and stopped against my shoe.

My mind blank, I stood still, staring at the two dead bodies lying at my feet, while the scorching sun burned my scalp and the wailing sound of police sirens rose in the distance.

PEST CONTROL

Kathy Kingston

All of my bouquets had sold except one. I'd had a good day. Pedestrians were few and far between, and the setting sun was casting a pink glow over the streets of downtown Los Angeles. Time to go.

And then that icy sensation traveled down my spine, and my head snapped up. Oh, shit. He's back. I knew even before my cat hissed. Goddammit.

Datura stared across the street at the athletic-looking middle-aged guy in black pants and T-shirt. He had thinning hair, aviator sunglasses and was smiling at me. It wasn't a nice smile, and he was pointing with both hands at his thigh. Reminding me that I was responsible for the probable mass of scar tissue there. We had some unpleasant history, and he had a long memory.

This wasn't our first go-round. He had stalked me before, but I lost him by slipping into crowds. Sometimes I cut through buildings or busy markets to avoid him.

But not today, I decided as I studied him. Today would be different. Really, I gave him every opportunity, but the scumbag just wouldn't give up. Not unlike my dear departed stepfather, pious and full of smiles, until we were alone. I tolerated him for the longest time because of my mom. Then, one day, right after I turned seventeen, I stopped being tolerant and I had to leave town, quickly. Make that very quickly. Maybe her new husband will be better. Probably not. She's way too needy.

Now, here, eight hundred miles away, yet another predator has me in his crosshairs. And, if he's anything like my stepfather, he won't give up easily, or at all. Which made my decision all the easier.

Someone was leaving the building behind me, and I turned. I like to make eye contact before I start my sales pitch, but the forty-ish woman in a business suit moving on leaden feet never looked up. She looked like she'd had a very bad day.

As she walked past me, I said, "Here, take this. A present for you." I handed her the last bouquet.

She paused, looking at me with apprehensive eyes.

"Really?" she said as she lifted the flowers to her nose. "These are lovely, thank you so much." The Double Delight roses still smelled amazing, even if they were starting to wilt. She needed them a lot more than the few dollars they might bring.

"Your cat is beautiful. Is she full-grown? "

"Yes, but she had a rough kittenhood. I found her half dead in a gutter two years ago. She didn't grow much."

"What's her name?"

"Datura," I replied. "It's a poisonous, hallucinogenic plant with a beautiful flower."

"Odd name."

"Yes; it fits her."

"May I pay you for this?" she asked, holding up the bouquet.

"No, it's a freebie."

Datura turned her head and growled.

The woman looked over my shoulder, following the cat's gaze.

"There's a creepy-looking man across the street, staring over here."

"I'm keeping an eye on him," I said.

She touched my shoulder and said, "Be careful. You're a young, pretty woman out here all by yourself, and he looks…menacing."

"Oh, and thank you," she said, holding up the flowers as she walked away. "I really needed this."

I get my flowers from the L.A. Flower Mart where I help take care of the feral cats that control the rodent population. Damage had become a thing of the past and customers seemed to enjoy seeing the cats. The flower mart and I have an unwritten agreement, and in exchange I take what I want from the discards. Recycling the flowers into pretty bouquets with ribbons, fabric, and other decorative trash made me feel good. I worked for myself, set my own hours, and it was an all-cash business. Life was good, but you still had to be careful.

A few months ago, my stalker attacked me from behind and dragged me behind the dumpsters. Luckily, I had my flower knife in my hand so I just stabbed and stabbed whatever I could hit until he let me go. His leg got cut up pretty bad and he left a nice-sized blood trail behind as he limped away down the alley.

Now he was across the street and looking for payback.

A shame I missed that damned femoral artery.

And then he was gone from sight. But I knew he wasn't really gone.

I gave Datura a good head scratch, then tucked her into the hood of my sweatshirt and headed toward Chinatown.

Twilight was coloring the sky lavender behind the silhouettes of construction cranes and skeletal bones of new buildings that dotted the skyline near and far as I walked through the city.

Gentrification was rampant and the L.A. economy was doing just fine.

I turned and scanned the shadows behind me. Nothing. Yet.

I headed east.

Finally, I passed through the Dragon Gate, grateful that this area was staying much the same. The smells, colors, and essence of Chinatown swirled around me as I walked toward Alpine Street. Storefronts covered with whirligigs, hats, fans and tassels crowded the sidewalks.

Passing a live poultry market, I stopped to watch an escaped chicken being pursued by a guy wearing rubber boots. There were several vehicles to hide under, and so far, the chicken was winning. I wished it good luck as I left.

I checked the street behind me. Still nothing.

Streetlights were popping on as the cool nighttime air settled around me. Normally I would stop for dinner. But not tonight. I paused, searching the shadows, but no warning bells went off. I almost felt disappointed. Datura wanted down so I put her on the sidewalk.

We headed toward the L.A. River where crumbling factories and gritty industrial sites loomed in the shadowy darkness.

The recent wave of urban renewal hadn't lapped at this particular shore yet. The area was bleak and ominous, but this was my home turf. I had been here long enough to know the lay of the land. I felt safe.

A full moon was rising. I stood in the glow, waiting, and then, there it was…

Datura hissing, and that feeling. A true, physical thing. That sixth sense that sent tingles down my spine. I knew exactly where he was. I turned in his direction as he stepped out of the alley and strode toward me with a triumphant leer.

I patted my Mace, scissors, and flower knife in my pocket for reassurance, but they were strictly for a worst-case scenario. I didn't intend to let him get close enough to have to use them.

"Datura, let's go." I headed quickly into the deep shadows puddled at the base of gloomy buildings. Footsteps echoed loudly behind us.

I started to jog as I got closer to the concrete ravine they call the L.A. River, cat running at my feet. The forbidding outline of an abandoned factory surrounded by chain link loomed in front of me. My destination.

Ducking down the alley beside it, I pulled open the loose corner of the fence, slipped through, then climbed through a gaping empty window.

Moonlight illuminated large pieces of machinery, wood, and trash scattered about the floor. Metal cables, ropes and chunks of old ceiling dangled from above. Bats flapped away into the darkness. The loud, metallic clang of chain link announced his arrival. I knew he wouldn't give up. I ran through the familiar maze, ducking and jumping over debris. I could hear him stumbling after me, cursing when the sound of his flesh hitting metal and wood echoed through the dismal space.

I ran up the rusty decaying stairs, his footsteps loud on the metal steps behind me. He was faster than I would have thought. I had lost track of Datura downstairs, but I knew she could take care of herself. Total darkness surrounded me as I reached the third story landing and stopped. So did he.

No windows. No light. I couldn't see him, and he couldn't see me, but I could hear his labored breathing close by. I reached out for the handrail, which guided me to a piece of chain on the floor. I kicked it. It was my early warning system.

"So, there you are," he said.

A great open darkness lay in front of me. Unhooking the rope that was curled around a beam by the handrail, I grabbed it in both hands and jumped. I sailed across the open space and landed on the other side. As I hooked the rope over a beam, I heard him kick the chain, so I knew exactly where he was.

"You cut me up bad bitch. Real bad. I coulda died. But hey, I forgive you. Let's talk. Where are you?"

Flicking my lighter on, I said, "Here, shithead."

He took a step forward, then yelled, "Fucking cat, go away." There was hissing, scuffling, then a loud scream as he turned and fell into the gaping elevator shaft in front of him. His piercing shriek ended suddenly as he hit the bottom with a loud thud. The giant piece of machinery below probably didn't help break his fall, it being all jagged and shit. The light had knocked out his night vision.

"Datura," I yelled. I was afraid she had gone into the hole with him, but she crossed over the opening on a beam and curled around my legs. I picked her up and we did a head bump. "Good job, partner."

Tomorrow I'll close the elevator shaft doors. Luckily, they work manually and it's only until the smell subsides. I have a bag of lime right next to the bag of kitty litter for just this situation.

We entered the large room behind me, and I flipped on the lights. No windows here either, but my home was cozy, thanks to "borrowed" electricity. It was perfectly safe too, as evidenced by my stalker and the other asshole at the bottom of the shaft. I looked around in appreciation. I had a good life, an excellent accomplice and a job I really enjoyed.

Exterminating vermin made the city a better place for everyone.

THE CASE OF THE ICE CREAM BLONDE

A.P. Jamison

The Paradise studio executive assistant exhaled, got up from his immaculate Hollywood desk and said, "Come with me," like this was the last thing he wanted to do. He smelled of too many stale cigarettes and too much cologne, and a touch of too little empathy.

I looked at my aunt, Miss Lemon Meringue Pie, and she nodded that it was okay to go with him. My golden retriever Marshmallow and I followed him to another office. The dang room was almost as big as the state of Texas.

Okay, I exaggerate a little, but the place looked more like an apartment than an office. It even had a wine and coffee bar, a conference table that easily sat fourteen guests for Thanksgiving, and a bathroom complete with a walk-in shower. A shower! Is that what studio executives did all day—drink wine and coffee and take showers?

It was 101 degrees out and, allegedly, unseasonably hot for Los Angeles. My aunt had already dragged my dog and me to Disneyland and back. My cowgirl boots hurt. I was itching for a lick of cool air conditioning, a good book, and some ice-cold water. Texas is hot, but somehow all this cement made California feel hotter.

The studio assistant stopped at the office door. He stared at my Stetson hat like it was an unforgivable fashion faux pas and said, "The executive in this office is currently on paternity leave, so for the next hour the office is all yours, but keep it clean." Then he promptly turned around and disappeared out the door.

Hollywood sure was a long way from my Texas ranch and this eleven-year-old cowboy boot-wearing, pecan-pie-loving, private detective cowgirl was plum tuckered out. Though I was still a little miffed that the studio wouldn't allow my aunt to bring me to the set. No kids allowed. The nerve. I wished we could've gone back home or at least to the hotel so Marshmallow and I could go back to the case we were currently working on.

But I loved my aunt something fierce. She had been my guardian ever since my parents had passed away two years ago, so I had to remind myself that this was what I needed to do to support her, especially since she had always supported me.

See, I got bullied a lot from the kids at school. They hated me because I was eleven going on forty, thanks to my vocabulary and I.Q., the fact that my family had money, though I didn't, and well, I wasn't very good at making friends...unless they had four legs.

So, Miss Lemon was always trying to cheer me up, hence this boondoggle to L.A. I didn't have the heart to tell her I'd rather be back home. I was no Cinderella. Not at all. I lived in jeans and boots. I had prison-bar-like braces, a long, blonde ponytail, big green eyes and a face I was told I needed to grow into. I mean, what the heck was that supposed to mean?

The sun blazed through the floor-to-ceiling glass window. I peered out between the hazy curtains. It was an epic Hollywood view, I could even see the sign, but Los Angeles seemed to be all cars and no cattle.

I just didn't feel right sitting at an empty desk that wasn't mine, so Marshmallow and I headed to the oversized sofa to the right of the desk. Behind the sofa was a movie poster for Agatha Christie's *Evil Under the Sun*. I liked this executive.

A succession of dainty knocks came from the open office door while I plopped down on the white sofa and Marshmallow curled up next to my feet.

"Hello, hello," said a deep, velvety voice that clearly had some formal vocal training.

I looked up to find a tall, twenty-something woman dressed in a metallic, blue-sequined evening gown with a matching cape, blue silk slippers, and a faux fur coat. She was staring with a fixed gaze at my dog and me. She also wore about $100,000 dollars worth of fake diamonds. What? I'm a Texas girl. We can spot fake diamonds all the way from Dallas. But here is the weird part...

Though Marshmallow was trained as my bodyguard, he didn't growl. Instead, he got up and sniffed her. Dogs possess 300 million olfactory receptors in their noses, while we humans possess only six million. Then he almost grinned at her and she ruffled his blond face fur. If she was okay by Marshmallow, she was okay by me.

Then she looked from my dog to me and flipped back a strand of her platinum blonde hair. "My, my, studio executives are getting younger and younger every year."

Was she putting me on? "Um..."

She broke out into a wide, perfectly white smile. "I'm only kidding. But I do have a question. 'How many people died in Hamlet?'"

"Nine," I said immediately, liking test questions...but wait a minute, had she somehow known that one of our last cases was finding out who murdered an actor during a production of Hamlet in San Antonio? Let's see. "How many do you think died in the play?"

"I happen to think that Ophelia's death might not have been an accident," she said.

Okay, maybe this was a coincidence, but I didn't believe in coincidences, so I continued, "I agree. Queen Gertrude was the last person to see her alive and she didn't want Ophelia marrying Hamlet. And Ophelia's death took place off screen, I'm just saying."

"Really?" She beamed and rested her head on her white-gloved hands. "Interesting. Leave it to William."

It was like she was on a first-name basis with Mr. Shakespeare, but he had been dead since April 23, 1616. Was this an L.A. 'thang?' "Are you a fan of Mr. Shakespeare?" I asked.

"Yes." She sat down in the pristine, white chair facing me. "Most people here in La La Land don't know who Hamlet is, much less who wrote it or how many people were murdered in the play. Now, how many sisters did Elizabeth Bennett have?"

"That's easy," I said. "Four."

"Name them."

"Jane, Mary, Catherine, but they called her Kitty, and Lydia. They lived at an estate called Longbourn."

She clapped her large, gloved hands together. "Oh good. Now, I was wondering if I could pitch something to you?"

What was up with her? Did she mean literally or metaphorically? I glanced at Marshmallow, who was still just calmly watching us.

"I mean a story. I want to pitch a story idea to you. I'm a bit nervous and I need the practice."

"Me?" I said. "You do know that I'm eleven?" I pointed to Marshmallow. "He's three."

"You are well-read; you appreciate a good story, and I hear you're a private investigator."

Like I said, there is no such thing as a coincidence. "How do you know that?" Marshmallow and I weren't here on official business.

"In this town, we dine on gossip."

"That doesn't sound very tasty," I said, suddenly craving some crispy Texas tacos.

She laughed. But it was a soft and sad and lyrical one. "Some days the gossip is just juicy and other days it's a kick to the gut."

"Jeez." It was very clear I was no longer in Kansas or Texas.

"I want to pitch you a story to see if you can figure out who did it?"

"You mean, a 'whodunit?'"

"Yes."

"Yippee." I was all ears, elbows and eyeballs now. Suddenly being at the studio was sort of fun, but still in a weird sort of way.

"Okay, I'll tell you a story and you see if you'd want to buy it?"

"You mean the person who normally sits in that chair," I said, glancing back at the studio executive's chair. "He sits and listens to people tell stories all day long and gets paid for it?"

"Yes, and he get paid lots and lots of money."

"On the ranch, we don't get paid money for telling stories, we get s'mores."

"Oh, you are so cute, I could just hug you."

"Hmm, I'll listen to your pitch, but please try and not turn me into fresh squeezed orange juice. Marshmallow *will* bite you." And he would.

"Deal," she said, slapping her knee ever so carefully so as to not hurt a blue sequin.

That seemed to be the word of the day in this town. What *was* the deal?

She put her hands on her knees. "The working title is *The Case of the Ice Cream Blonde.* Then she pulled her hands together. "Imagine. The year is 1935, here in Hollywood."

"Wasn't that Hollywood's Golden Age, where the studio system ruled, so five studios controlled the whole film industry?"

"Yes," her blue eyes widened, "very good. Now, picture it." Her gloved hands formed a giant frame. "You're a 29-year-old, famous actress, a beautiful, blonde bombshell, who has one-hundred-fifty film credits to your name. You've even worked with Laurel and Hardy."

My face must've gone blank. I needed to work on that because she said, "You don't know who they are, do you?"

I shook my head. "I know The Hardy Boys, but go on."

"Okay. You've also opened a successful restaurant called The Sidewalk Café at 17575 Pacific Coast Highway in the Pacific Palisades. That was a big deal for a woman back then. You have money coming in from your films and your restaurant. You're in the middle of filming a movie called *The Bohemian Girl.* You have a wide circle of friends and associates and nothing in your life suggests that you would have a reason to end your life."

I pulled out my iPhone from my jeans pocket and opened "Notes." It always made clients feel better that I took notes, and she was suddenly sort of a pro bono client, even if it was just a "pitch."

"Then," she paused for effect, "at approximately ten thirty on the morning of December 16—again, this is 1935—you're found in your garage slumped over the steering wheel of your brown Lincoln Phantom convertible."

"When you say slumped, I'm dead?"

"Very dead."

"What day was December 16?" I asked.

Her thick but perfectly waxed eyebrows furled. "It was a Monday."

I needed a timeline of events.

"And just two days later, on December 18, 1935, the coroner ruled your death a suicide from carbon monoxide poisoning."

"You don't think it was suicide?"

She put her hands on her hips. "No, I don't."

"Had I finished making the film?"

"No. And you had a substantial role. All your scenes had to be reshot. And as a professional actress, I think you would've at least waited until you had finished shooting."

"Did I leave a note?"

"No, you didn't. See…"

"Unfortunately," I said, "per the National Library of Medicine, only a minority of suicide victims, varying between 3-42 percent, leave notes."

Her gloved hands went silent.

"But," I said, "it's case-by-case. And you think I would've left one?"

She nodded. "I do. Besides, your mother said you were not suicidal."

"Well," I said. "There are four types of death. Suicide, murder, misadventure—which means by accident—and old age. Since I was just 29, I think we can rule out old age...even here in Hollywood."

"You're funny," she said. "In a good way."

"What was my name?"

"Thelma. Thelma Alice Todd. And your nicknames were Hot Toddy and The Ice Cream Blonde."

"Who would've wanted me dead?"

"You mean suspects?"

"Yup." I loved me some suspects.

"First, there was the ex-husband, Pat DiCicco, who you were married to from 1932 to 1934. He was a movie producer, as well as being a mob enforcer for the crime boss Lucky Luciano."

"Why the heck did I get involved with him?"

"You knew how to pick 'em."

"Well, boys gross me out so I'm not picking any of them. But point taken. Now, regarding my death, data from the U.S. Crime Reports suggest that about one in five homicide victims are killed by an intimate partner."

"Good Lord!" she said, leaning back in the plush chair.

I nodded. "The police always start with the spouse or partner. Crimes of passion are way too common."

"Now I understand how you passed the SAT with a perfect score at ten years old."

How the heck did she know that? I wondered.

She eyed me. "You do your homework and so do I."

"Okay, then, why don't you suspect the ex-husband?"

"The night before, you had run into each other at a party, but you left the party in your chauffeur-driven Lincoln around 4 a.m. in good spirits, but still a little drunk. Then, you headed up the steps to your apartment alone for the very last time."

"That makes me sad."

"Tell me about it. It's a heartbreaker."

"What about my mother?"

"Your mother thought you had been murdered and never believed it was suicide. You were cremated, and after your mother's death in 1969, your remains were placed in the corner of her casket and buried in Bellevue Cemetery in Lawrence, Massachusetts. Do you think that would've happened if she had murdered you?"

"Jeez." I shook my head and my ponytail swished between my shoulders. "Did I have any injuries?"

"The coroner only found a contusion on your lower lip."

"That's still something. It could have been from a slap or even a punch to the lip."

"I know. Rumor is that it was much worse."

"Could it have been a robbery gone bad and staged to look like suicide?" I asked.

"You were found wearing exactly what I am wearing now, except your fur and diamonds, worth a whopping $20,000 back then, were real."

"Who else was I close to?"

"You had a maid named Mae Whitehead, but she had no motive to kill you. In fact, it was Mae who discovered your body that morning. Poor thing."

"Was the garage door locked?"

"No."

"Who else had a motive?"

"Well, your business partner in the restaurant was a movie director named Roland West."

"What was Mr. West like?"

"He was jealous, possessive and had a bad temper. A very bad temper."

"So, he was controlling?"

"Yes. And you lived next door to each other."

"I sure knew how to pick 'em," I said. The blonde bombshell

nodded and then glanced away. "What aren't you telling me?" I asked.

"Back then, in the golden age...well, let's just say it wasn't always golden for women, especially actresses. Many were treated like men owned them."

"And you think he killed me?"

"I don't know what to think."

"When was he notified of my death?" I asked.

"That is a very good question. The Los Angeles County sheriff's detectives went to Hal Roach's studio on Tuesday to tell him that you were dead. He was the producer on the film."

"Did he have a motive?"

"No. Just the opposite. He had to reshoot all your scenes, using another actress. Even back then that was the last headache a producer needed."

"So, Mr. Roach was told this news the day *after* I was found dead?"

"Yes."

"What was Mr. West doing on that Monday?"

"All day when people called for you, he said he didn't know where you were."

I sighed. "Given how jealous and possessive he was and given that he thought I was going back out again that night, if he really hadn't known where I was, wouldn't he have been calling all over town trying to find me?"

She jumped up. "Yes!" She leaned back in her chair and closed her eyes. "But he was a very, very powerful man."

"Powerful enough to get my murder covered up?" I asked. I, too, was not happy about this.

She nodded and then whispered, "There was already another big scandal back then and Hollywood only likes scandals if they are selling tickets."

"Meaning it would have been bad for show business?"

"Yes. Very bad. You were a big star and Roland West was a big director."

"Would Mr. West have gone to jail for this crime back then?"

"That's the thing. He would have had the very best lawyers and he would have denied everything. There was no evidence. And actors aren't the only good liars in this town."

"And there were no witnesses?"

"None."

"That worked in his favor."

"But how do you think he did it?" she asked.

I let my mind wander for a moment to put the pieces of the whodunit puzzle together. Then it all clicked. "First, as you said, it was 1935. There were no TVs, much less shows like CSI back then. If Mr. West and I were fighting, maybe when I left and got into my car to get away from him, to go to another party, he could have locked the garage on me. Men like that always want to teach women a lesson by not letting them go. He probably got so mad he wasn't thinking about carbon monoxide poisoning, and neither was I, and I was still a bit drunk, too. Then, he could've waited for me to sober up and cool off, or he finally cooled off and went back later and found me dead in my car. He then left the garage door unlocked this time and waited for the maid to find me in the morning. If he was my business partner and living next door to me, he knew my routine and my patterns."

Tears pooled in her eyes. "So, he may have really gotten away with murder..."

I glanced behind the credenza. *The Scream*, by Edvard Munch was hanging on the wall behind it. I suddenly wanted to scream in anger. She was right. Thelma Todd may have been murdered.

I pulled out a fresh tissue from my backpack, and I said in my kindest voice, "We will never know. But jail is only one sort of prison. If he did contribute to 'my' death, that is in itself its own sort of hell... I wouldn't wish that on anyone."

The studio assistant suddenly appeared at the door and looked at this blonde bombshell sitting in the chair across from me, weeping onto her metallic blue sequined evening gown, and said, "Hey Movie Star, John Davis-Downer needs you to go to the canteen and get his lunch." Then the assistant pulled a Houdini and disappeared again.

I had to pull my chin up from the floor. Again, I exaggerate just a bit. "Is it still 1935 around here?"

"On some days, it sure feels like it."

"How is it you're pitching to studio executives and getting them lunch too?"

Her laugh turned wry. "I'm just a studio intern."

"Intern?" I was reduced to word repetition.

Then she got up and wrapped her cape around her shoulders as if it could somehow protect her from Hollywood and evil. "I now believe that Thelma Todd's death was accidental, or she was murdered by Roland West, and he got away with it because, thanks to the golden age of Hollywood, he had the power to cover it up."

"But," I said, "we'll never really know. That happened ninety-seven years ago. Mr. West died on March 31, 1952. I just looked it up. Unfortunately, all involved are now dead, too. Why is this case so important to you?" I asked.

She grabbed the door handle and turned to face my dog and me like she was Hollywood royalty. "Because I always wanted to be her growing up. She's my idol. Now thanks to you, I too believe that Thelma didn't commit suicide and I find comfort in that."

"No one should ever get away with murder, not even here in Hollywood," I said. Marshmallow barked as if in agreement.

"Kid, Hollywood is wild and wonderful, but it is also weird, wicked, and worm-filled."

"You're the best part of Thelma now."

"Am I?"

"You're keeping her memory alive."

"I am? I am." She broke out in a smile. "Promise me you'll stay true to your cowgirl boots and ranch roots and go back home to Texas."

“You betcha. We cow-folk are ruled by a moral code. It’s just how we roll.”

“Good, I think I need to meet more cow-folk in this town, but right now I have to go fetch his lunch…”

“Good luck,” I said. I was sort of sad to see her go. “You’re more fun than any amusement park. And it’s a dang good pitch in my humble pecan-pie opinion.”

“Thanks. By the way, what’s your name?”

“Augustus,” I said, “but I prefer Gus. And you?”

“It’s Todd,” she said using her natural man’s voice. “But you already knew that.”

I nodded. Of course, I did. The height, hands, eyebrows, legs and the deep richness of the voice. I’m a detective, but I’d get grounded if I had asked. We all have our secrets, and my aunt would say it was none of my beeswax. Besides, I hate wearing dresses, especially pink ones, so who was I to judge what anyone else wore.

Todd continued, “People tease me and call me Hot Toddy or The Ice Cream Blonde, but in honor of my idol, friends call me Thelma.”

“Nice to meet you, Thelma.”

Source: *Who Killed Hot Toddy? The Mysterious Death of Thelma Todd* by Benjamin McVey.

OVERHEATED

B.J. Graf

Cat Gutierrez pressed her Nike-clad foot down on the accelerator of the silver Toyota Prius as she hugged the curves on Malibu Canyon. It was 7:15 p.m. on a hot, humid Friday of the Memorial Day weekend and she was heading east toward the 101. Cat's last job had taken a little too much time, so she'd had to book the red-eye from LAX with two stops to Cabo. Her family was gathering in Mexico to celebrate her father's sixtieth birthday. Cat hadn't seen her dad since COVID shut everything down, and she could not miss the flight.

Cat had taken extra work on in order to get Dad the special watch he'd always wanted—a Rolex Oyster Perpetual Datejust with its deep marine blue face. She reached into the front pocket of her carryon and pulled out the timepiece, holding the box aloft so she could admire the brand's crown logo before setting it on the passenger seat beside her. Cat hadn't had time to wrap the box, but she could imagine her father's expression when he opened the gift. How his brown eyes with the tiny gold flecks would widen with pleasure, the little lines at the corners crinkling as he beamed. How surprised he'd be. Men always underestimated her abilities—even her own father.

Let's just see what her brothers got Dad this year. Cat smiled as she imagined their reactions.

It was magic hour. The day's light was fading fast, but as she motored through the canyon, Cat could still see how the sun had already fried spring's greenery on the surrounding mountains, bleaching everything to a parched burnt umber.

She steered the Prius, with its hybrid engine doing its tepid best, from Malibu toward the Valley. The speedometer read fifty mph—a little fast for the canyon with its hairpin twists and turns and the steep drop on her right, but she was in a hurry to get to LAX.

Cat glanced in the rearview mirror and straightened the few errant strands of the wig's straight shoulder-length black hair that had come loose. A gold clip held the rest in a neat bun at the nape of her neck. Her twenty-seven-year-old face with its tilted brown eyes over high cheekbones looked a little tired, but nothing a nap on the plane couldn't cure. The gray jumpsuit she wore for work still looked pretty fresh.

Cat barreled through Calabasas as the terrain flattened out and Malibu Canyon Boulevard turned into Las Virgenes. Two service stations selling gas at the all-time high of seven dollars a gallon flanked the entrance to the 101 South just up ahead. She'd make good time on the freeway and leave the car in long-term parking at LAX, where the client would pick it up. Cat turned onto the freeway and floored the gas, smoothly making her way to the fast lane before the next exit.

On the radio the talk show host with a dire cast to his baritone voice said, "Violent crime rose 22 percent from 2020 to 2021. Murders shot up from 355 to 397 in the same period, and folks, it looks like 2022 will beat those numbers." He nattered on. Smash and grab burglaries, robberies, assaults, homicides—apparently all categories of crime were up. Times were tough. Cat turned off the radio.

The speedometer read seventy-five now as the traffic thinned out. A black Porsche and a gray Tesla passed her going at least ninety, but Cat didn't take the bait. Let them race. No point in going faster and having the CHP stop, ticket her, and make her miss her dad's big day. She kept her foot steady on the gas as the dark gray ribbon of freeway spooled out before her.

And then suddenly Cat felt the power in the hybrid engine go. She pressed her foot all the way to the floor of the Prius, but the car didn't accelerate. No power. Nothing. The car was coasting.

Cat slammed on the hazard lights and turn signal as she steered to the right. She dodged the cars whizzing past in the other lanes. Horns blared as drivers honked and gave her the finger. She took a deep breath as she made it to the slow lane. An exit was directly ahead. Cat took it, coasting to a dead stop on the right side of the offramp. Her hands felt like they'd been welded to the steering wheel. Cat pried them loose and took a few more deep breaths, forcing air into her lungs.

There were no streetlights on this offramp. The Prius's hazards were still blinking but on this moonless night it was getting dark fast. Cat hoped the other cars speeding past could see her in the gloom. She didn't want some drunk driver to slam into the rear of the Prius.

She thought about calling AAA, but the wait on a holiday weekend could be long. The 101 had cameras like most everywhere now, but Cat didn't see any on this exit. The CHP might not spot her sitting here in the dark. Cat pulled out her phone and texted a friend from work who lived fifteen minutes away. He was a gearhead who had every automotive tool, including one of those little self-contained battery chargers.

What's up? Juan 'Big Dog' Campos texted back a few minutes later.

A favor, Cat texted back. *Prius broke down. Help?*

Out of gas?

One of the things Cat really liked about Big Dog was his cut to the chase competence.

No. Cat's thumbs flew across the phone's keyboard. The gas tank showed three quarters full.

Overheated?

No, again. The thin red line lay halfway between hot and cold on the dash gauge. *It's weird. The engine stopped dead. Battery?*

That is weird. Need a charge?

Can you? Cat texted him the offramp.

15 minutes, Juan texted.

I owe you.

No worries, he texted back.

Fifteen minutes.

Cat unhooked her seatbelt and knuckled the knots in the small of her back. She made herself stretch and then began to surf social media while the minutes ticked by. Cat checked local crime news first. Nothing of interest surfaced. That was reassuring.

On Twitter and Instagram, her eyes quickly glazed over at the two hundred heart emojis and gushing "love it!" posts in response to a selfie pic of breakfast by some trending blonde cookie-cutter-pretty teen. That was a lot of passion for a plate of pancakes. There were equally heated negative posts about everything from gun violence and abortion rights to the latest TV show that disappointed fans of the book the series was based on. And passengers on Southwest Airlines were throwing punches over carryon space in the overhead bins. Tempers ran hot everywhere, and it seemed to Cat that people were losing it. Emotional outbursts were as inflated as the soaring gas prices. The whole country was breaking down.

She glanced at her phone. 8:05 p.m. She still had time.

Then the flashers on the Prius began to sputter, fade, and die. Great. Dark settled around the Prius like a blanket.

"Shit." Cat's stomach began to sink. She might miss her flight after all. Or worse. Those crime stats she'd heard on the radio earlier buzzed in her head. These days you couldn't be too careful.

Cat texted Juan again to let him know she was sitting in the dark, no flashers to show her position now.

Sorry. Late start he texted back. *Had to take a call.*

Fewer cars drove by now. And the day's oppressive heat had started to lift.

A black Chevy Equinox with tinted windows exited the freeway and headed toward her. The SUV slowed down as it passed, then sped away. At least it didn't hit her.

Five minutes later the Equinox was back. It had those headlights that looked like cat's eyes, and the silver rim around the grill that resembled a smile. The black behemoth exited the freeway and slowed to a stop twenty feet from her Prius. A Good Samaritan? Or the opposite?

The driver of the SUV got out and slowly headed toward her. He was a wiry twenty-something guy of more than medium height and indeterminate race with short black hair. He wore a white T-shirt and baggy jeans that hung below his butt, revealing red briefs. No weapon as far as she could tell.

"Hey, you okay?" Red-briefs-guy flashed Cat a big smile. He had very white teeth. "I saw you were stuck here so I circled back. You by yourself? You need help?"

Maybe he was a nice guy. There were still a few nice guys out there.

"It's okay," Cat said. "I already called for help. They're coming."

"Yeah? How far away? It's not good for a pretty lady like you to be sitting here alone in the dark." He kept coming closer until he was only a foot or so from her door.

"Thanks anyways, but I'm good." Cat tried to start the Prius again. Nothing. Still no power.

"You better let me help," he said. "The cops don't come by here very often." His smile broadened.

How would he know that? The hairs on the back of her neck prickled.

Her heart beating faster, she rolled up the window and made sure the door was locked.

Eyes trained on Red-briefs-guy, Cat knocked the unwrapped Rolex box off the passenger seat and onto the floor, but she saw his eyes widen as they fixed on the expensive timepiece.

"Just a second." He leaned down as if to tie his sneaker, but when he stood back up, there was a six-inch-long rock with a jagged edge in his right hand.

It happened fast.

The window's safety glass crumpled into a thousand tiny pieces.

She popped open the glove compartment, scrambling for anything she could use to defend herself, tossing aside the box of disposable latex gloves she used for work.

He reached in, opened the door and started to drag her out. "Gimme the Rolex."

"Please. Don't. It's for my father."

"Buy him another one. You don't do what I say, I'll smoke you, bitch." He reached into the car, grabbed her by the back of her neck and pushed her down toward the floor of the passenger side. "Gimme the Rolex. Now."

He was too big to fight, and Cat didn't think she could outrun him. She handed him the watch. Red-briefs-guy tucked it into a jeans pocket. He took her phone, too, then dragged her outside the car and over to the passenger side. Throwing the door open, he started to rummage through her carryon. He tossed her heels and the dress she planned to wear to her dad's birthday party onto the dirt.

"If you don't take the watch," she said forcing a calm into her voice. "I'll give you my purse instead."

He paused and stared at her, then smiled again. An unpleasant smile that said, *Stupid bitch, I'll take both.* "Where's your purse?" He started to rummage through her things again. His right foot carelessly ground her dress into the dirt as he upended her carryon and dumped the rest of her belongings out onto the side of the road.

"What?"

"Your purse. Where's your purse, bitch?!" The guy began to scream at her, his voice an unhinged screech. He grabbed her arm again, his fingers digging into Cat's flesh. Then he slapped her.

"In the trunk." Cat could feel her face turn red and hot where he'd slapped it. But the rest of her had gone numb.

"Open it." He shoved her back toward the drivers' side.

"Hurry up."

"Okay, okay." Cat reached in and pulled the little lever on the driver's side. The trunk popped open. He hauled her toward the rear of the car, smirking. Her Nikes dragged a little on the pavement.

He opened the trunk, and the smirk died on his lips as he stared at the contents inside.

At the bloody corpse tucked into a fetal position on top of the dark plastic painter's tarp. The dead man's eyes had clouded over to cataract-white, and blood had dried around the neat bullet wound just below his left ear.

Red-briefs-guy's mouth fell open. His shock and the moment of hesitation were all Cat needed. She reached past him to the small gap between the dead guy and the side of the trunk. The dead man's gun in her hand, she fired a shot in Red-briefs-guy's face. He dropped like a boneless fish.

One less thug in the world. Like all the scumbags she'd been hired to wipe out. Her employers didn't call Cat to take out nursery school teachers.

Cat glanced around. These days, there was always the danger that some looky-loo with a cellphone would shoot a video he shouldn't, but it was a risk she'd had to take.

Blood and brain had spattered on the rear of the car. She'd have to clean that up.

Slipping on a pair of latex gloves, Cat took back the Rolex then fished the keys to the SUV with its blackened windows from the jeans pocket of the now-dead robber. She turned the Equinox around and moved it close so both cars were trunk to trunk. After putting down a fresh tarp, Cat dragged both corpses into the SUV one by one. She crammed them together like twins in the womb and laid more of the plastic over them. She'd really need a back massage after this job.

Cat retrieved her now-soiled belongings from the side of the road and stuffed them back into the carryon. She had silver-sparkle leggings on under the jumpsuit. She'd buy a dress for the party at the airport terminal. Cat stowed her carryon in the floor space on the passenger's side.

Then Cat broke down the Glock used to kill both thugs and cleaned each part, wiping off any trace of prints. A glance confirmed that the serial number had already been filed away and acid-washed. She would toss the pieces of the Glock out the Equinox's window every few miles on the way to the airport. She knew where the cameras were and weren't on the route.

She also wiped down the steering wheel and all parts of the Prius she'd touched. If anybody reported the abandoned hybrid before she could arrange to have it picked up, the Prius would be clean. She'd do the same to the Equinox when she parked it in the long-term lot at LAX. Cat didn't worry about leaving hairs because of the wig. She'd toss that at the airport, along with the gray jumpsuit after she was out of sight of the cameras. Cat had already scoped out a blind spot near the ladies' room on the arrivals level. The client's clean-up squad would do a more thorough job when they retrieved both cars.

Cat texted twice more. Once to Juan to cancel and thank him. And another to the clean-up squad to tell them they'd need to pick up two vehicles instead of just one, together with the location of both cars. The phone was a burner purchased for cash and all her texts were encrypted, but Cat still pulled the SIM card and smashed it with the thug's rock. She'd dump the phone too.

Cat started the car and drove off, the engine purring. She glanced at the time on the dash: 8:45 p.m. Late, but no reason to get overheated. The Equinox had muscle. Cat would make her flight, and Dad would be so thrilled when she put the new Rolex on his wrist.

THE BODY IN THE BARREL

Kathy Norris

Ned Jenkins steadied himself as he walked the rim of the hip-high wall around Lake Henshaw Dam. It was 8:00 a.m. on a...what day was it today? Wednesday? Thursday? He took a swig from his twenty-five-ounce can of Bud, the aluminum cool against his sweaty palm. His vintage *Playboy* baseball cap shaded his seventy-two-year-old eyes from the sun, but his flip-flops were so hot they scorched his feet.

What day was it, again? He swayed slightly, almost losing his balance as the hot breeze ruffled his Hawaiian shirt and Bermuda shorts. He'd retired eight months ago and hadn't been able to keep track of the days since.

"The booze is pickling your brain," he recalled his know-it-all spouse Sandy saying earlier today. Ned took another sip of Bud. What did she know? If he was an alcoholic, would he be able to walk the wall like he was now? He held up his arms as if balancing on a tightrope, beer in hand. One misstep, and he'd tumble down the incline to the water's edge.

A dog began barking wildly. Ned whipped his head around, trying to identify the location of the sound. The next thing he knew he was falling, tumbling head over heels toward the shoreline. He came to rest spreadeagled on his belly in the mud, staring into the bowels of a corroded fifty-five-gallon industrial barrel.

The rusty, misshapen container rested on what had once been

the bottom of the lake. But the worst drought in California's recorded history had drained the man-made reservoir to 30 percent of its capacity, exposing the mud-covered barrel to the pitiless sun. Its lid was missing, so Ned could see inside. *What the...?* He looked closer. Something looked back. Bones. A skeleton. The empty eye sockets of a human skull.

Detective Pace, single mother and seventeen-year veteran of the San Diego County Sheriff's Department, parked her unmarked Dodge Charger at the crime scene. The light falling on the barren landscape reflected only three colors—the muddy brown of the lake bottom, the cobalt blue of the lake, and the thin light blue of the sky. A panorama of vast, primordial emptiness. Against this backdrop the tangle of brightly colored news vans and reporters stood out like a rash.

Chet Jones of San Diego Fox 5 was the first to pounce. "Detective Pace, what do we know about the homicide?"

"Who said it's a homicide?" Geneva didn't break stride.

"Is it true that the lower the water level, the more bodies may surface?" This, in breathless Spanish, from Leslie Martinez of Univision.

"Me estoy enfocando en este cuerpo," Geneva replied. *I'm focusing on the body at hand.*

She ducked under the crime scene tape as though she had her teenage daughter's knees. Only when she was facing away from the reporters did she wince. The crime scene tape kept the media and looky-loos about twenty-five yards from the barrel, which rested a foot from the water's edge. Geneva didn't recognize the first officer on the scene, so she kept her eyes trained on his face as she introduced herself.

"Detective Geneva Pace, Homicide."

And bingo, there it was, that quick shift of the white rookie's eyes to the left as he absorbed three essential facts: she was Black, she was a woman, and she was his superior. His eyes shifted back to her face quicker than most.

"What've we got here, Officer Cotton?" Geneva asked, noting his name and badge number.

"At 8:43 a.m., I responded to a call from dispatch, possible 10-54, dead body at Lake Henshaw. The individual who made the call, Ned Jenkins, was on scene when I arrived at 9:17. I inspected the barrel and called homicide and the evidence techs. I secured the crime scene at approximately 10 a.m., pending your arrival."

Geneva nodded her head. "Good job." She surveyed the crowd, which seemed to have doubled since she arrived. They'd probably come from the group of houseboats tied to the pier upriver. "Call in for additional crowd control. Where are you holding Jenkins?"

The rookie pointed to a white-haired man standing apart from the crowd. He wore a muddy Hawaiian shirt and flip-flops, and held a can of beer in his hand. Budweiser. "I told him not to talk to anyone until you arrived."

Geneva walked over to Jenkins. "Ned Jenkins? Detective Pace. You called this in?"

Jenkins looked her over, his sunburned skin flushing a brighter shade of red. His eyes darted left and stayed there.

"Yessh." Geneva clocked the faint slurring of his words. His eyes returned to her face, his lips upturned in a wet smirk.

Like most detectives assigned to the coroner's office, Geneva wore a dark polo shirt with her name, *G. Pace, Detective,* embroidered over the right pocket. The word SHERIFF was printed in large yellow block letters on the back. Dark cargo pants and sturdy footwear completed the ensemble. Thank God she no longer wore a uniform. If she had a dime for every middle-aged white guy who cast her in his Cleopatra Jones or Foxy Brown fantasies... She flipped open her notebook and gave Jenkins her best Taraji P. Henson scowl. That usually sobered them up.

Jenkins pointed to the pier where several boats were docked. "Last one on the end. Mine."

Geneva put on her sunglasses and looked at the boats through her new progressive lenses. It took a moment, but she found the sweet spot and read the jaunty names painted on their sterns. The LIBERTY. The GALE.

"The SHIP-FACED is yours?"

"Mine," he repeated.

Of course it is, Geneva thought.

"You figured that out...smart cookie." Jenkins grinned. "Like that lady detective on that old TV show, *'Get Christy Love.'* You look like her...the lady detective."

Geneva rolled her eyes. Teresa Graves, the Black woman who starred as Detective Christy Love, stood five-ten and had been a model before becoming an actress. Geneva was five-two, could stand to lose a few, wore her hair in a severe bun and didn't even own lipstick. Chapstick didn't count.

"Sir, I'm not here to discuss 1970's blaxploitation films," Geneva snapped. "Tell me about the barrel."

Jenkins straightened up. "I walk the lake every morning." He gestured to the calcium deposits that formed a bathtub ring around the basin. "Water hit a new low. That's when I saw the barrel." No need to mention his ignominious tumble.

"What time was this?"

"Eight o'clock or so. I looked inside and saw a human skull. Nearly shit my pants."

"Did you touch the barrel?

"Nope."

"Did anyone else?"

"Nope."

Geneva flipped the notebook closed. "That's all for now, Mr. Jenkins. I'll need you to come in and give a written statement." She handed him her business card. "Anything else you want to add?"

"Nope."

"Thank you."

Geneva walked away. Her junior partner, Detective Travis

Smith, had arrived and was standing next to Officer Cotton. Travis raised his hand in greeting, his lady-killer blue eyes hidden behind mirrored aviator sunglasses.

"Hey, Detective!" Jenkins yelled.

Geneva didn't turn around. *Wait for it*, she thought, *three, two, one...*

"You're under arrest, Sugah!" Jenkins howled, using Christy Love's signature catchphrase.

Geneva flipped Jenkins the bird without breaking stride.

Travis, who'd seen the whole thing, grinned as Geneva approached. "Another fan?"

"Bite me. Ready to walk the scene?"

The squad had nicknamed Geneva and Travis "The Odd Couple" for good reason. She was short and round, a Black woman born and raised on the liberal west coast. Tall and skinny, Travis hailed from Arkansas. He'd voted for Trump in 2016 and doubled down in 2020. They had originally been paired as a joke, management hoping the constant chafing of their differences would make Geneva quit. But when Travis had been falsely accused of a federal crime, Geneva had stood by his side. Today their homicide clearance rate was second to none.

Geneva and Travis pulled on gloves and circled the barrel without touching the surface. It lay on its side and was covered with so much mud Geneva couldn't tell its original color. Raised rings circled the exterior, dividing the barrel into thirds. Time and corrosion had worn holes along one side. The entire container was warped, as if an angry Hulk had picked it up and repeatedly bashed it against the ground. Geneva, hands on knees, inspected the lid, her face inches from the surface.

"There are some letters stamped on the lid." She traced them with her gloved finger, careful not to touch the surface. The indentations were so slight they barely registered. "A.P. Do those letters mean anything to you?"

"No," Travis said.

Geneva peeked inside the barrel while Travis activated his cell phone flashlight and illuminated the darkness inside. All soft tissue had decomposed, leaving only the skeleton behind. What looked like a human skull was clearly visible, lying atop a pile of bones.

"See that?" Travis pointed to a hole about the size of a marble in the frontal lobe.

"Gunshot wound," Geneva said. "Homicide."

"So, what do we know?" Geneva asked Travis as they grabbed a late lunch at Subway. Travis bit into his footlong Spicy Italian with extra pepperoni, salami and bacon ranch dressing.

"The HMS Cholesterol is going to send you to an early grave." Geneva nibbled at her tuna salad.

"With a smile on my face." Travis finished the first of two bags of Lay's Classic potato chips. "We've got a body in a barrel. Identity unknown. Gender unknown. Date and manner of death unknown. Motive unknown."

"Possible gunshot victim. If the bullet lodged in the soft tissue of the brain, it probably stayed inside the barrel after the body decomposed. With any luck the evidence techs will find it."

"The victim didn't shoot himself and put his own body in a barrel," mused Travis. "Feels like a professional hit to me."

Geneva nodded. "If this was Lake Mead near Las Vegas, I'd say it had mob written all over it. Is the mob changing it up, dumping bodies in San Diego now?"

"Awfully risky, killing someone in Nevada and transporting the body over state lines to California."

"Then there's the barrel itself," Geneva said. "Joe Blow doesn't have access to fifty-five-gallon steel drums. Probably a local source. Put together a list of local industries that use fifty-five-gallon barrels."

"It's going to be a long list."

"Narrow it down to the top three industries in San Diego: defense, especially the submarine and shipbuilding yards...pharmaceuticals. Skip tourism and technology—the tech boom's fairly recent..."

Travis looked up to see Geneva frowning at her low-fat baked potato chips.

"Why doesn't Subway sell Fritos?" she asked.

"To piss you off."

"It's working."

Geneva pulled into her underground parking space. A red and white Mini Cooper was parked next to her. Zoey, her sixteen-year-old daughter, was home.

"It's me!" Geneva announced as she entered the front door of the three-bedroom condo she shared with Zoey. She sniffed the air. *What was that smell? Burnt garbanzo beans?*

She set her keys next to Zoey's on the mantlepiece. Her eyes lingered briefly on the framed photograph resting there: Geneva cradling an infant Zoey in her arms, next to a young, Black soldier in combat fatigues. At the bottom of the frame were inscribed the words:

Anthony Wayne Pace
1st Armored Division—Iraq
1983-2005
Gone But Not Forgotten.

"I'm in the kitchen," Zoey called out. "We're having vegan macaroni and cheese for dinner."

Geneva stifled a groan. "Sounds delicious, hon," she said, sorting through the mail. A bill from San Diego Gas & Electric. Flyers from local businesses.

Geneva carried her daughter's mail into the kitchen, where Zoey was elbow deep in pots and pans. It looked like every mixing bowl, measuring cup, and spatula in the condo was spread out on the cooking island.

"What can I do to help?" Geneva asked her daughter.

"Chop the tomatoes for the salad."

Geneva rinsed them in the sink and diced the tomatoes like the sous chef she once was. The knife flashed as she worked.

Zoey put the casserole in the oven and sat down to sort through her mail. "Finally," she said, inspecting one of the envelopes.

"What?"

"The DNA test kit from Ancestry-dot-com is here. For my science project."

"The family tree assignment?"

"Yeah, it's due, like yesterday. I already uploaded our family tree online. Now I need to send a DNA sample. My friend Debbie found a sixth cousin on her mother's side she didn't even know existed on Ancestry-dot-com."

It occurred to Geneva that the public had access to DNA analysis tools just like the coroner's office. "How do they get the DNA?"

"You spit into these sample tubes." Zoey opened the envelope and retrieved the vials. "Then mail it off to their lab. Can you put them in the mail at work tomorrow? I got one for you and one for me...hey, Mom!" Zoey leaped from her chair and hurried to Geneva's side.

"What?" Geneva held the knife in mid-air.

"You cut yourself," Zoey said, pointing to her mother's left hand. Geneva followed her daughter's gaze. Drops of her own blood, as bright and red as the tomatoes, dripped onto the white cutting board.

"No biggie," Geneva said. "Get the first aid kit, will you?"

The doorbell rang while Zoey bandaged her mom's finger. "It's Uncle Phil," Zoey said. "I invited him to dinner."

Geneva smiled. Philip Bell had been her late husband's best friend and was like a brother to her. "Don't keep the man waiting. Open the door before he finds out you're feeding him rabbit food."

The next morning, Geneva carried the Ancestry.com mailer

containing the DNA samples into the office. Instead of mailing it, she locked it in her bottom desk drawer.

"What can you tell us about the body?" Geneva asked forensic pathologist Michael Villaroman. She and Travis were in the pathologist's autopsy suite in the San Diego Coroner's facility.

Dr. Villaroman removed his eyeglasses and rubbed the bridge of his nose. He turned to his computer monitor and rattled off information.

"Body found at Lake Henshaw on Wednesday, April 27, 2022, at oh-eight-four-three hours. The body was received in an advanced state of decomposition, with no soft tissues available for analysis." He looked at them. "That makes determining the cause of death difficult. Without fingers, we have no fingerprints to establish the victim's identity. Without a throat, we can't tell if the victim inhaled mud, and therefore was alive, when they entered the water."

"What about the hole in the head?" Travis said.

"Examination of the skull identified one bullet entry wound. No exit wounds, but we did find a bullet casing in the barrel, consistent with the damage to the frontal lobe." He scrolled to a new page. "I took a sample of the bone marrow from the femur and analyzed it for diatoms, or microscopic algae that would appear only if the victim had drowned. No diatoms were present. My preliminary conclusion is death by gunshot wound, prior to entering the water."

"Bottom-line it for me, Doc," Geneva said.

"Based on the shape and size of the head and pelvis, dental wear, and analysis of the length of the femur, your victim was male, between twenty and thirty years old, and between five-four and five-eight in height. Given the level of skeletonization, he's been under water forty to fifty years."

"Between 1972 and 1982," Geneva said. "We'll start with the missing person cases going back to the 1970s."

The pathologist nodded. "We've got DNA and dental imprints from the skeleton. If you identify a potential victim, we'll confirm one way or the other."

Geneva and Travis headed for the office they shared with the other detectives. The room was strictly utilitarian: thin gray carpet, white walls, shaded windows. The administrative support sat in the back. A conference table in the middle of the room held a surprisingly healthy plant and a bucket of Red Vine licorice. A life-sized skeleton with a military helmet perched on its head stood next to the communal refrigerator. The detectives' metal desks were scattered throughout the room, the surfaces cluttered with monitors, printers, office supplies, files, coffee mugs, crumpled lunch bags, and prescription medications. The detectives had plastered the walls alongside their desks—those not already covered by bland artwork—with case notes, maps of the county, and business cards for restaurants that delivered twenty-four seven.

Travis's desk faced Geneva's. A fan of the *Rocky and Bullwinkle* television show, Travis had decorated his space with cutouts of Rocky the Squirrel, Natasha and Boris Badanov, and the talking moose, Bullwinkle, himself.

Geneva's desk was the cleanest in the office.

Travis fired up his desktop and navigated to the County Sheriff's crime database, then searched for open missing persons cases in San Diego County. Geneva looked over his shoulder. There had been two since 1967.

"One woman and one man," Travis said. "The missing man's name is James Hurley."

The file contained a photo of a white male in his early twenties, dark brown hair cut short on the sides and long on top. Brown beard and moustache. An easy smile.

Geneva leaned in closer. "What's that on his neck?"

"Looks like a tattoo. A Coptic cross."

Geneva nodded. "What else we got?"

Travis scanned the file. "Hurley drove an eighteen-wheeler for Associated Packaging, the container company. Boxes, metal drums, plastics, and whatnot. Five will get you ten that the initials A.P. on the barrel stand for Associated Packaging."

"I don't bet. Especially not with you. Keep going."

"The A.P. warehouse manager, Russell Gibbs, logged Hurley in around seven on the night he disappeared. Hurley went to the Spotted Pony bar after his run. The bartender said Hurley closed the place, drunk as a skunk. Gibbs reported him missing when Hurley missed a couple days' work. The police found Hurley's pickup truck abandoned near a lagoon in Oceanside, but no Hurley."

"Any dental records?"

Travis scanned through the medical records. "Not on file."

"Contact A.P. and ask for his medical records. Maybe we'll get lucky. In the meantime, let's visit Russell Gibbs."

Travis powered his souped-up Camaro along the I-15 North to Russell Gibbs's address as identified in the police report. Geneva sat in the passenger seat.

She eyed the speedometer. "You know the speed limit is sixty-five, right?"

"It's safer for everyone if drivers with superior reflexes drive faster."

Geneva snorted.

Russell Gibbs lived in one of Escondido's middle-class neighborhoods in an off-white duplex with an adobe tile roof. A petite woman with a tumble of graying curls answered the door. She smiled at them with the confidence of a woman used to turning heads.

"Good afternoon, ma'am." Geneva showed her badge. The smell of baking filled the air. "We need to speak to Russell Gibbs."

"I'm his wife, Charlotte." The woman beckoned them inside. "Russell," she called out, "the police are here to see you."

"Bring them to the kitchen," a male voice shouted with the urgency of a doctor delivering a baby. "My soufflé is almost done."

Charlotte led the detectives back to the kitchen. Geneva recognized the hallmarks of the serious amateur chef: Julia Child's "Mastering the Art of French Cooking" lay open to the Soufflé au Fromage page. A mound of gruyere cheese sat next to the grater. Russell even had Crème of Tartar to stiffen his egg whites. The chef himself wore an apron streaked with flour. He smiled at them through wire-frame glasses as silver as his hair. Geneva estimated him to be a spry seventy-something.

"My apologies." Russell Gibbs offered them his hand, then retracted it to wipe the flour off before extending it again. "Soufflés are so finicky. They'll collapse if you don't pull them out at exactly the right time. How can I help you?"

Geneva decided to cut him a little slack. Whose heart hadn't been broken by a collapsed soufflé? "We're following up on a missing person investigation."

Russell blinked. "James Hurley. Well, who else could it be?" he said in response to Charlotte's soft gasp. "He's the only missing person we know."

"Tell me about Hurley," Geneva said.

"We're talking forty, maybe fifty years ago. Russell Hurley came back from his round-trip to San Jose, went to the Spotted Pony and was never seen again."

"How well did you know him?"

"Not well. He'd only been with us for a couple of weeks before he disappeared. You found him?"

"We found a body matching his general description," Geneva said.

"Where?"

"Lake Henshaw."

Charlotte's eyes filled with tears. "Poor man."

Hurley pulled his wife to his side and gave her a gentle squeeze. "There, there, pet."

For a moment Geneva wondered how different her life might

be if Anthony had survived Iraq. If she'd had a partner to share life's burdens.

"How did he die?" Charlotte asked.

"Bullet to the head," Geneva said.

Charlotte flushed. Russell turned pale.

"Why that's...that's just terrible," Russell said.

"Did he have any friends at the warehouse we should talk to?" Geneva asked.

"He and another driver started working for A.P. the same day. Tony or Toby Harris, something like that. You didn't see one without the other."

"There's no mention of Harris in the file," Geneva commented to Travis as they headed back to the office. "See if you can track him down."

In the next few weeks Travis pulled out all the stops in his search for Harris but came up empty. The traditional missing person searches—hospitals, jails, homeless shelters—yielded nothing fifty years after the crime. "It's like he disappeared off the face of the earth."

"Patience," Geneva said. "You've planted the seeds, let them grow. Where are we with Hurley's dental records?"

"Still waiting on the court order. I'll keep you posted."

Three weeks later Geneva was leaving a crime scene when her cell phone rang. It was Travis's distinctive ring tone, the *Rocky and Bullwinkle* theme song.

"You'll never guess where I am," Travis said when she answered.

"The Burning Bush?" Geneva named a local strip club.

"No, although that's not a bad idea. On my way to Los Angeles to get a bead on Toby Harris. I got a hit with NamUs." NamUs was the National Missing and Unidentified Persons System database. "Apparently he, or someone using his social, enrolled in a substance abuse program in North Hollywood."

"No shit."

"Shit," he said. "And it gets better. I gave A.P. my cell as a contact for Hurley's dental records. The secretary called me. They're ready for pickup."

Geneva pumped her fist. "Solid." She did a U-turn in the middle of the street and headed for the freeway. "You track down Harris, I'll pick up the records."

The Personnel Department secretary wasn't having it. She sat in front of the Personnel Director's office, eyes narrowed, arms crossed. Brewer, the Personnel Director, was not in.

"The records are on hold for Detective Travis Smith," the secretary told Geneva.

"Detective Smith is my partner."

"Per company policy we can only release the records to the originator of the request."

Geneva stifled the impulse to tell the secretary where to shove company policy. The secretary looked pointedly at her watch and, rising, pulled a paper bag from beneath her desk. Noon. Time for lunch. Per company policy.

"Policy is policy," Geneva said, faking a small, defeated voice. "Do you mind if I use your bathroom?" Gracious in victory, the secretary donned her sunglasses and pointed to the ladies' room on her way out the door.

It was the work of an instant for Geneva to nip back down the hall and slip inside Brewer's office. A large envelope with the words "Hurley" sat in his outbox. Geneva scooped it up and was about to make her getaway when she saw the photographs on the wall behind Brewer's desk.

The wall was covered with company bowling team photos. The largest was a 1972 championship photo featuring a trophy bigger than the Superbowl Lombardi. The names of the participants were captioned below. Brewer was hoisting the trophy in the air, Russell Gibbs at his side. On Brewer's other side, his arms around Brewer's shoulder, was a familiar face. Narrow, with dark brown moustache and beard. A Coptic cross tattooed on his neck. James Hurley.

"Russell Gibbs lied to us," Geneva shouted into her cell phone as she maneuvered the Dodge along the I-5 after leaving A.P.

"Come again?" Travis was on the other end of their bad connection.

"When we interviewed Russell, he said Hurley only worked for A.P. for a couple of weeks. But Hurley was a member of the bowling team long enough to win the league championship. He's in the championship photo."

"What else is Gibbs lying about?" Travis wondered aloud.

"Toby Harris. He probably doesn't exist, just some name Gibbs made up to send us on a wild goose chase. It always bothered me that Harris wasn't mentioned in the detective's report."

"Son of a bitch. I'll head back now. ETA three or four hours with all this traffic."

"I'm on my way to Gibbs." Geneva ended the call and stepped on the gas.

The first heavy drops of an unexpected thunderstorm were falling when Geneva arrived at the Gibbs home. Charlotte Gibbs answered the door.

"Russell's not in," she said.

"I'm here to see you, not Russell." She showed Charlotte the bowling team photo she had taken from Brewer's office. The one of Brewer, Gibbs and Hurley holding the trophy. And seated behind them, Charlotte Gibbs. But Charlotte's eyes weren't on Russell. They were on James Hurley.

"You'd better come in," Charlotte said. Thunder boomed overhead.

"Why didn't you say you knew Hurley?" Geneva followed Charlotte into the kitchen where she had been fixing dinner. Baked chicken, canned green beans and mashed potatoes. Russell, not Charlotte, was the gourmet in the Gibbs household.

Charlotte flashed Geneva a look before she began quartering the chicken. "How many women do you know talk about their affairs in front of their husbands?"

Fair point, thought Geneva. "Tell me about your relationship with James Hurley."

Charlotte fell silent, the only sound the rain drumming against the roof. "I thought we were in love," she said at last. "It was madness, I know. I was married to Russell. Not happily, mind you. Not then. I was young. You know how it is. Pretty and clueless. Thought the grass was greener on the other side. Jamie and I were going to run away together that night. But when Jamie didn't show up, I went back home. And there was Russell." She swallowed hard. "Cleaning his shotgun at the kitchen table."

"He what? And you never thought to ask…"

"Said he'd been out hunting with friends," Charlotte continued. Her eyes met Geneva's. Tears began to stream down her face.

"So, you're saying you never thought Russell murdered your lover? Even after seeing him with a gun? Even after Jamie clean disappeared and the police started investigating?"

Charlotte smiled, but her eyes glistened with unshed tears. "I'm the only woman Russell ever loved. I mean, what if my affair with Hurley drove him over the edge? But then I thought, not my Russell. He's such a pussycat. I figured that Jamie had just run off, so why was I getting myself worked up? The affair seemed less real with each passing day. After a while, it was like nothing ever happened. Like I never cheated or anything bad happened." Her eyes stayed on Geneva's. "Sometimes we believe what we need to, right?" Her mouth twisted into a wan smile.

"What happened to the gun?"

"Russell still has it." Charlotte was silent a moment. "Russell probably thought Jamie's body would never be found. But secrets don't stay buried, do they?" Her eyes bored into Geneva's.

"No, they don't," Russell spoke from the kitchen doorway.

Both women jumped. Neither had heard him enter because of the storm. The genial senior-citizen baker was gone, replaced by a dead-eyed killer pointing a shotgun at Geneva's head.

Geneva abandoned the idea of drawing her gun before it fully formed. Gibbs would get off a shot before she even touched her weapon.

"Put your gun on the kitchen table," Russell ordered Geneva.

"Don't make a bad situation worse." Geneva slowly pulled her handgun from its holster and placed it on the counter. Gibbs's shotgun didn't waver. She needed a distraction...

Charlotte clenched her fists. "You killed Jamie." It was not a question.

Eyes pleading, Gibbs turned to Charlotte. "I had no choice..."

His split-second of inattention was all Geneva needed. Quick as a flash, she snatched the chef's knife Charlotte had been using to cut the chicken and hurled it at Russell. It flew end-over-end and buried itself in his shoulder. With a cry he dropped the shotgun and clutched his arm. Geneva kicked the weapon out of his reach.

"Call nine-one-one," she commanded Charlotte. She retrieved her own weapon and trained it on Russell.

Weeks later Geneva arrived home to find Zoey burning something in the kitchen. Wistfully she recalled the delicious smells coming from Russell Gibbs's oven. Not that he'd do much cooking in prison. Russell Gibbs had confessed to murder. The James Hurley missing person case was closed.

Riffling through the mail, Geneva found an envelope from Ancestry.com. Probably the results of the DNA test kit she'd retrieved from her desk and mailed the day after Gibbs's arrest. She fingered the envelope, stomach clenched. She had a choice. Tell her daughter the truth or continue to hide the fact that the man in the photo on the mantelpiece was not Zoey's father.

But secrets don't stay buried. Even if it hurts, you owe the truth to those you love.

"Zoey." She carried the Ancestry.com envelope into the kitchen. "We need to talk."

THE REGULAR

James Thorpe

Palm Springs, 1967

Ray listened to the ice tinkling in his glass as he swirled the amber fluid around and around, the frozen cubes glinting in the glow from the candelabra. He leaned his elbows on the drink-stained grand piano, feeling the thrum of the hammers striking strings beneath the closed lid, beating out a tattoo of "Moon River." Why did that song always make him so sad? And just what the hell was a "huckleberry friend," anyway?

"Two bits for your thoughts."

Ray looked up from his glass to the blonde pianist, Veronica. "Two bits?" he asked. "What happened to a penny?"

She inclined her head toward an ashtray where smoke curled up from her burning cigarette. "Luckies are twenty-five cents a pack now."

"Yeah...well, everything's going up. Inflation, they say."

Veronica finished playing, flashed a mischievous smile in his direction.

"All I know is it's getting harder and harder for a working girl to have any vices left."

Ray saw his face reflected in her dark glasses, the curve of the lenses distorting his features like a funhouse mirror. His attempted smile looked more like a grimace of pain.

"Still blue?" she asked.

"You a mind reader now?"

"I don't wear these shades 'cause I'm deaf. Whenever you've got something on your mind you twirl that glass of yours. Makes the ice sound like tiny bells."

Ray put down his glass. His restless fingers probed a blackened scar on the piano lid.

"And the last couple days you started scraping your fingernail over that cigarette burn in the piano top."

Ray stilled his hand. "Guy can't have any secrets around you."

"Do you have any secrets, Ray?"

"Me? Nah. Too boring, according to my wife. Ex-wife." Even as he said it, it didn't feel real yet. When would the shock wear off, and reality kick in?

Veronica said, "Oh, I doubt that." She reached out toward the ashtray that was in the same spot it always was…right above the middle C key. Ray watched her slim fingers pluck the lipstick-stained cigarette.

"Those things'll kill you."

A cloud of smoke billowed from her red lips. "So can a lot of things. Cousin of mine once ate some bad shrimp in Tijuana. Keeled right over. And just last week, you hear about that drunk who fell into the pool at the El Mirador?"

Ray shook his head, then, remembering she was blind, said, "Uh-uh."

"Nobody found him till morning. Poor bastard. You never know." She struck a few notes of the "Funeral March" to underscore her point. "I mean, hell, sometimes just crossing the street…"

Ray's hand twitched, knocked his glass over. "Shit." He grabbed a cocktail napkin to stem the flood of single malt.

Across the dimly lit lounge the bartender, Jake, called out, "I got you."

Ray was glad Veronica couldn't see his cheeks flush crimson.

"Want to talk about it?" she asked.

"You already know the story. I don't want to bore you again."

"C'mon, we're friends, right? Besides, you're a good guy."

"I'm a chump."

"Not true. But even if it was, nobody deserves to get shafted like that."

Jake appeared beside Ray, deposited a fresh drink.

"On the house, buddy." He clapped him on the back. "Look like you could use it tonight." Before Ray could mumble, "Thank you," Jake drifted back toward the bar, his footsteps swallowed up by the thick red shag. For the first time Ray noticed the carpet was the color of blood.

He took a sip of fresh scotch. The fire coursing down his throat cleared his head as it always did. At least for a while.

"Nine years," he said. "Then one day I come home from work, find her bags packed by the front door. She says she wants more. I'm not enough. Then she's gone."

"I'm sorry. Tough break."

"Maybe there were signs..." Ray shook his head slowly. "How could I not have seen it coming?"

"When the heart's involved, maybe we're all a little blind."

Ray looked up to see Veronica smiling sadly in his direction. Her dark glasses caught the reflection of the candelabra, giving her flames for eyes. He shivered, took another drink.

"You know, Ray, maybe you want to take it easy on the joy juice."

"What?" Ray asked. "You disapprove?"

"I'm just the piano player."

"Sure. Why should you care?" The comforting glow of the alcohol was slowly giving way to the icy fingers of self-pity. "Not even my own wife cared about me."

"Maybe she didn't see you like I see you."

"Yeah, right."

"Maybe she didn't understand you."

"And you do."

"Well...I know there's more to you than meets the eye."

"That's a strange choice of phrase."

"See, I know what you're capable of."

"Meaning?"

"Two nights ago."

Ray's hand jerked his glass to his lips again. Damn thing was still empty. He signaled Jake who called out, "Gotcha, buddy!"

Ray cleared his throat. "What do you mean about a couple of nights ago?"

Veronica's fingers danced lightly over the keyboard. "You killed a man."

He gazed into the flame-eyes reflected in her dark glasses. He couldn't speak.

Veronica said, "Saw it with my own two eyes." She pulled her glasses down the bridge of her nose. Her eyes were a bright, almost luminescent, blue. One eye winked at him. It felt like a gut punch. "Yeah, not blind. And by the way," she pointed at Ray's jacket, "third night in a row for that beige corduroy jacket. Doesn't really do much for your complexion."

A vise tightened around Ray's throat. He struggled to speak. "I don't...why...?"

"The glasses?" She shrugged. "Just part of the act. Guys think it's sexy. They get to stare at my chest without getting caught. Plus, the tips are better. Everybody feels sorry for the blind girl."

"But that's..."

"Dishonest?" She grinned mischievously. "You're a fine one to talk." She slid the glasses back on.

Ray jumped as Jake materialized at his elbow with a fresh drink. "Steady, tiger. To your health." He looked at Veronica. "You good, V?"

She smiled. "Never better."

Jake moved off.

She said, "Hey, I'm sure you didn't mean to do it."

"What? No. Of course not."

"That old guy shouldn't have tried to cross against the light.

But it was after two in the morning. He probably thought it was safe. Not usually any traffic on Sonora at that hour."

"You saw?"

"I'd just gotten off work, was walking home. I guess the poor bugger must've been deaf, too, not to hear you screech around that corner. Man, that was quite a *thunk* he made, bouncing off your hood."

Ray tried to swallow, but it was hard with that vise still tightening around his throat.

"If it's any consolation, Ray, he died instantly. At least, by the time I got to him, he was dead. 'Course, you wouldn't know that, the way you sped off. Without even stopping to check on him or call an ambulance."

Ray gulped his scotch. "Why…why didn't you…?"

"Call the cops? 'Cause we're friends. Ever since you started having trouble with the little missus and coming in here regular, telling me your sad stories, I've become kind of attached."

Ray took a deep breath, but the air scraped and scratched on the way down like he was swallowing dead leaves.

Veronica said, "One thing I'm wondering…even before you hit him, you were driving like a bat out of hell. Where was the fire? Were you drunk?"

But Ray wasn't listening. "You're not going to tell anyone? Really?"

"Cross my heart and hope to…well, you know." She segued into "But Not for Me," and smiled up at him. "You're not a bad person. You just made a mistake. We all make mistakes. And besides, like I said, I'd hate to lose a regular customer."

Ray licked parched lips. He looked at his empty glass. He had to slow down. He needed to think.

Veronica said, "I notice you're driving a different car."

"Jenny's. My wife's." He blinked. "Ex-wife's."

"She didn't take it when she left?"

Ray shook his head. "I'd bought it for her as a birthday present. She said it would always remind her of me. Wanted a clean start."

"What a bitch. Smart of you to swap cars, though. There could be traces of blood or skin on yours."

A young couple holding hands entered the bar. They paused a moment, waiting for their eyes to adjust to the murk, then crossed to a corner booth.

Veronica smiled. "Young love."

Ray watched the couple for a moment. He tried to call up memories of Jenny and him when they were young and still in love. But the past was still blurred with present pain. The fights, the screaming. The way she looked at him like he was pathetic. Like if she didn't hate him so much, she might even feel sorry for him. He shrugged off the memory, pushed his empty glass away. "I should slow down. If I get pulled over now, it wouldn't be good."

"I think that's smart."

"So, you may not see me for a while."

"Oh, no. Don't say that."

"I'm not talking forever. But as long as I'm not drinking...I might as well just not, you know, drop by. At least for a while."

"Ray, I'm afraid I can't let you do that. You're a regular now."

Ray tried to laugh, but it came out as more of a yelp. "Nah, I'm serious."

"So am I. If you stopped showing up, I'd miss you. And I'd miss your tips." She nodded toward the large brandy snifter stuffed with dollar bills. "Although I have to say, lately, you've been a little stingy. That's going to have to change."

A damp, creeping cold tickled his armpits. "What do you mean?"

"Just what I said. I want to know you appreciate what I'm doing for you by not telling the cops what happened. I want to see you start dropping some bigger bills in that tip glass."

"But that's..."

"Let's call it an ongoing contribution to my musical appreciation fund."

"Whatever you call it, it's still blackmail."

"Oh, I see." A sly smile. "Just like hit and run is still murder?"

Across the lounge, the young couple were laughing and kissing in the booth. The girl noticed Ray staring and said something to her boyfriend. Now they both turned to look at him. He felt like there was a giant spotlight pinning him with its beam. That someone had tattooed "MURDERER" on his forehead.

Ray could tell the boy was getting angry. He was probably thinking, *who the hell was this guy staring at my girl?* Another second and he'd be on his feet, headed for Ray. Eager to defend, to impress.

But right now, Ray didn't want any trouble. He couldn't afford to attract attention. He turned back to Veronica, who seemed to be waiting patiently for an answer.

"You're serious," he said.

She nodded. "My dream has always been to open my own place. Doesn't need to be as big as this. I'm not greedy."

Ray laughed a mirthless laugh. "Right."

"Just a nice neighborhood bar. Good music, good cocktails."

Ray couldn't believe what he was hearing. She actually was serious.

She said, "I realize this comes as a surprise, so we can start small tonight." She nodded toward the large brandy snifter serving as tip jar. "Let's start off with twenty. I'm guessing you've got at least that much cash on you."

He felt in his breast jacket pocket for his billfold. His fingers felt numb, disconnected from his hands, his body. He fumbled the billfold out, opened it. He counted out a ten, a five, a couple of ones. "Seventeen. That's it."

"Better than nothing. As my granny used to say, 'Great oaks from little acorns.'"

With trembling hands Ray stuffed the bills into the snifter.

"Thanks, Ray. Much appreciated."

"So now...what?"

"Tomorrow's Saturday, and the banks are open, so I'm expecting more from you tomorrow night."

Ray licked his lips. They felt like sandpaper. "How much?"

"I think twenty-five has a nice ring to it."

A shuddering sigh escaped his chest. "How long do you..." He couldn't finish the sentence.

Veronica shrugged.

"I don't understand," Ray said. "If you're going to blackmail me, just get it over with. Why are you dragging this out?"

"Because, sweetie, I've been watching Perry Mason for years. And blackmail's a crime. So is accessory to the fact, or after the fact... I can never remember which. Bottom line, I figure slow and steady is the best approach. 'Cause let's say a few days or weeks go by and the cops figure out it was you, your car, that killed the old guy. They arrest you, maybe even find out about our little arrangement. And boom, I'm going bye-bye, too."

"And this way you could always just claim I was a big tipper."

"Exactly. *Oh, that Ray. What a guy. Always throwing his money around, trying to look like a big shot. You know the type.*"

Ray was silent a moment, running the numbers in his head. Veronica seemed to read his mind.

"That's right, Ray...we're open six nights a week. Six times twenty-five is a hundred and fifty smackers."

"Every week? That's over...seven thousand a year."

"Seven thousand eight hundred, to be precise."

"But I'm barely clearing nine grand in salary now. Where the hell am I gonna come up with that kind of money?"

"Work harder. Ask your boss for a raise. You've been assistant manager for how many years now? It's time you got promoted."

"Christ, you sound just like Jenny."

"Well, Ray, ambition is not a four-letter word."

"This can't be happening." The tightness in Ray's throat spread down to his chest, constricting his rib cage. Is this what a heart attack feels like? At least that'd be one way out of this nightmare.

Veronica called over to Jake at the bar, "I think Ray's gone dry." Jake gave her a thumbs up, reached for the Johnnie Walker.

Ray heard a whooshing noise in his head. It sounded like his life being sucked down a sinkhole to disappear forever. "I can't..."

She wagged a warning finger at him. "Now *that's* a four-letter word." And with a sharper edge of steel in her voice, "I don't want to hear that word again. Ever."

"Then, Christ...I guess...I don't know. I'll...have to get a loan. Sell the house. My fucking house."

Jake materialized beside him with his drink. "Bottoms up, buddy." Then he noticed the overflowing tip jar. "Looks like you had a good night, V."

Veronica smiled sweetly. "It's always a good night when Ray's here."

Jake clapped Ray on the back and headed off. At the piano, Veronica swung into a jazzy version of "We're in the Money." And Ray lunged for his glass like a drowning man clutching at a life raft.

The Palm Springs afternoon heat was a branding iron on Ray's back as he pushed through the door, headed inside to the dark, cool lounge. To think this room and Veronica's music had once brought him peace, an escape from life in the outside world. But all he noticed now was how damp and dank the lounge smelled. Like a musty tomb.

She'd heard the door open and tilted her head in that way a blind person sometimes does when they hear someone enter a room. Even though he knew she could see him clearly through her dark glasses, she called out a tentative, "Welcome, welcome...

And who do we have here this afternoon?"

"Hi." Jesus Christ, he hated that bitch. "It's Ray."

"Ray!" She beamed. "Nice to have you back. Take a seat."

Ray circled the grand piano to his usual stool, and all the while her head followed him, the reflected candelabra flames blazing in her dark glasses. She looked like a blonde, female demon. *Maybe I'm already dead*, Ray thought, *and this is what hell looks like.* No sulfur and brimstone. Just the stench of stale beer and cigarettes.

Veronica lowered her voice. "Looks like you've lost a bit of weight, Ray."

"It's been a rough couple of weeks. Thanks to you."

"Oh, come now, you know you brought this on yourself. I just want you to eat right, take care of yourself."

"I'll bet you do."

A meaty hand slapped his back. Ray whirled to see the grinning face of Jake as he slid a scotch in front of him. "Hey, Ray! Keep this up, I'm gonna engrave your name on this stool."

Ray tried to smile, but his lips twitched as if he'd been electrocuted. He managed to mumble a half-hearted, "Yeah," before Jake went back to his bar.

Veronica paused to light up a fresh Lucky. "You asked your boss for that promotion yet?"

Ray shook his head. "Not yet."

"Why not?"

"You don't understand. It's not that simple." He sighed. "Jenny didn't understand, either."

"Sure, it is. You just walk into his office and say, 'Mr. Smith…I've been a loyal employee for' —how many years is it now, Ray?"

"Seven."

"Seven years. And sir, I feel it's time I moved up in the company."

"He doesn't like me."

"So what? He doesn't need to like you, just respect you. And how can he respect some guy who's willing to just punch a time clock, year after year, not displaying any ambition—"

Ray slammed his drink down so hard that an ice cube jumped out, slid across the piano top. "Shut up."

"Now, Ray, there's no call—"

"You're starting to sound just like Jenny again." His voice took on a high-pitched whining tone. *"You've got no gumption, Ray. No get-up-and-go. No drive."* He took a swig from his glass. "You don't know what it's like out there. Neither did she. First time I make one misstep, there are fifteen, twenty guys lined up behind me, ready to grab my job."

"Which is why you need to move up the ladder. Become a boss, not just an employee. Don't be a victim. Be a leader."

"You don't give a shit about me." He snatched his wallet from his jacket pocket, tore out a twenty and a five, jammed the bills into the tip jar. "That's all you care about."

"Since you brought it up, I think it's time we had a talk."

"You got no complaints. I've been keeping up my end of the bargain."

"True," she said. "It's been a couple of weeks now, and you've proven to be a man of your word."

"And I've been checking the papers, watching the news. There's been nothing since that first item after the...accident. I think the cops have moved on."

Veronica nodded. "It looks that way. Which is good news, for both of us."

"Why both?" Ray shot her a suspicious glance.

"I think it's time to increase your daily contributions from twenty-five to fifty."

"Fifty dollars? That's double!"

"Lower your voice, Ray."

He didn't realize he'd shouted. He looked around at the small, early afternoon crowd. Heads turned in his direction. He turtled down into his collar and glared at Veronica. "What the hell?"

"Don't get upset. I'm the one who's actually taking on more risk here."

"You?"

"Sure, it's been a couple of weeks and it looks like you got away with it…but there's still a chance—a slim one—the cops could find out. And as much as I think we make a great team, I don't want to get dragged down with you on a murder charge."

"My savings are empty."

"Then you'll need to get a loan."

"We already took out a second mortgage when Jenny decided she had to have a pool."

"So ask your boss for a raise, and a promotion. Show some ambition and all your troubles will go away."

Ray squinted at her, trying to pierce her dark glasses with the intensity of his gaze. But all he saw was his slouched, defeated reflection. If this was how he had looked to Jenny, no wonder she had kept harping on him. Christ, he was pathetic enough to turn his own stomach.

"If another few weeks go by and the cops still don't find anything, is your price gonna go up again? You going to force me to sell my house?"

Veronica shrugged noncommittally. "Let's cross that bridge when we come to it."

"What's to stop me from walking away from you and this shithole forever?"

"I'm a witness. I saw you kill a man."

"So what? Your word against mine."

"Evidence."

Ray asked, "What evidence?"

"Pictures of your car with that big dent in the hood."

"You broke into my garage?"

"The photos also show traces of blood and a few hairs. I scraped off some of the blood, took some hair. Got 'em safe in a Tupperware bowl in my freezer."

"You're a monster."

Veronica laughed lightly, dropped her hands to the keyboard. They began dancing to "Mack the Knife." "If you ask me, the true monsters are real estate agents. What is happening to prices in the valley? I've been checking out possible locations for my new lounge, you know, hoping I could stay in town. Bigger tourist trade, I think. But even if I rent instead of buy, I'm going to have to start looking out in Cathedral City, Rancho Mirage. Not ideal."

"My heart breaks." He raised his glass. Empty. He must've drunk it, but he couldn't remember.

"Ready for another?"

He shook his head, slid off his stool. "I'm done."

"For the *night*." Even through her dark glasses, he could feel her eyes boring into his.

"Yeah."

"See you tomorrow. And remember, it's time to double our fun."

Ray nodded numbly. "Sure." He stumbled to the door, pushed out into the early evening. Even though the sun had dropped behind the San Jacinto range hours ago, the air was still parched, heat-blasted. It would be hours more before the sidewalks and roads began to cool with the coming of night, and Ray could breathe. And think about what to do next.

At three a.m., the traffic on Avenida Palmera was nonexistent. Streetlamps pooled light up and down the block, but the only sign of life Ray saw was a skinny coyote slinking across the road in search of an early morning snack. Ray took a step back and stood in the shadow of a palm tree. Then he heard them.

Footsteps. Heels on cement. High heels.

He waited until they came closer...closer... and then he stepped out in front of Veronica. She wasn't wearing her dark glasses now, and he saw the surprise in her eyes.

"Ray? Little late for you, isn't it?"

"It is. I'm tired. So tired."

"You didn't hang around just to walk me home after work, I hope."

He reached into his jacket, pulled out his Colt Commander semi-automatic. The one he brought back from the war. It had saved his life more than once back in Saigon. And it was about to do it again.

"Jesus, Ray! That's a gun."

"Get over to the car." He pointed toward a brown Olds Cutlass.

Veronica's eyes darted back and forth. "Ray, c'mon..." He knew she was hoping someone would drive by or be looking out a window. She raised her voice. "This isn't you. Put away the gun and we can talk."

"Shut up. Move." He jerked the gun barrel in the direction of the Olds. Veronica walked toward the car.

Ray keyed the trunk, popped it open. "Get in."

Once again, she scanned the deserted street. "Look, honey, we can work something out. I know you. You're a good person. You just made a terrible mistake. Don't make an even worse one now."

Ray looked at her, realizing this was one of the few times he'd stood face to face with her, and could see her eyes. They weren't candelabra flames. They weren't even the eyes of a demon. They were just blue. Kinda bloodshot. And very scared. Strangely enough, that made the next bit much easier.

Ray lashed out, struck her cheek with the butt of the Colt. She yelped in pain. "I said, get in."

"Okay, Ray, sure...just take it easy." She clambered awkwardly into the gaping maw of the Cutlass, tearing a gash in her nylons. "But can't we at least talk—"

He shoved her head down and slammed the lid shut. Driving off down the street he heard the cries for help and the desperate thumping coming from the trunk. But he didn't care. He already felt free.

***

Headlights raked across the barren landscape, bouncing up and down as the Olds rumbled along the abandoned dirt track. Every now and then the lights would catch an ocotillo plant, its bright red flowers blooming like a bloodstain in the night.

Ray stopped in front of a rickety wooden hut with two walls collapsed, leaving it open to the elements like a lean-to. He got out of the car, opened the trunk, shone a flashlight inside. The beam's glare picked out Veronica's blonde hair and bare legs, stark white against the dark trunk liner. Her rumpled dress, now soiled with grease. A couple of broken fingernails, probably from pounding on the trunk. And finally, her face, makeup smudged from the spare tire nestled up against her. Even in her disheveled state, her eyes were still that beautiful luminescent blue. Blazing at him now with fury. And fear.

"Ray…I don't understand. You don't have to do this."

He hauled her out roughly by one arm. She skinned her knee on the fender, cried out. "We can work something out."

"You told me to take initiative."

"C'mon…this is a joke, right?"

"Just like Jenny. Always nagging. Going on and on about ambition. Never leaving well enough alone." Ray raised the Colt semi-automatic. He nodded toward the decrepit hut, now more of a lean-to. "Over there."

He could almost hear the wheels in her head turning. She looked around. Tried to change the subject. "Where are we? The desert?"

"Joshua Tree National Park."

Her eyes tried to pierce the gloom beyond the car's headlights.

"I don't recognize…"

He shoved her toward the lean-to. She took a stumbling step over the rocky terrain.

"This is the old mining area," he said. "Abandoned now.

They used to pull copper, gold, lead out of this dirt. Right up until the fifties; then the companies just walked away. Left all these holes in the ground. Deep holes." He prodded her again toward the lean-to.

"No, Ray! Please…I won't ask for any more money."

"Move!" Another shove. She was at the edge of the decaying structure now. Ray shone his light on the ground. Rotted wooden planks had been pulled aside, exposing a large hole in the ground. A former mine shaft. Descending into blackness.

Veronica panicked. "Please! I'll give your money back."

"*Stand up for yourself*, she said. *Be a man. Guess you can't*, she said. *Guess you're just too chicken shit.*"

"Ray, I never said those things."

Ray spun her around to face him.

She was starting to whimper now. Christ, he hated that sound. "Ray, you're not…you can't shoot me!"

"Of course not." His flashlight beam picked out the beautiful blue luminescence of her very wide, very terrified eyes fixed on the gun in his hand. "It was never even loaded." He rammed the muzzle into her chest. She stumbled backwards, heels teetering on the brink of the open mine shaft. A rotting board snapped under her weight…and she dropped from sight.

Her receding scream ended abruptly with a thud.

Ray stepped up to the lip of the shaft, shone his light down. Past the dirt-caked walls, down, down to the bottom. Seventy-five, maybe a hundred feet below. His light played around the black pit until it found a spray of blonde hair. She was still alive. Still whimpering. Ray noticed the way her legs bent at an odd angle, and guessed she'd broken her back. Probably shattered her spinal cord. Severed the nerves. Likely why she wasn't screaming in pain. Ah, well…small mercies.

He thought he heard her call his name. But Ray knew the desert can play tricks on you. Especially at night.

On the off chance she was still conscious he felt he owed her some explanation. He called down the shaft, hoping her ear drums hadn't ruptured in the fall. "You should've just left me alone. I don't want a promotion. I never did. I don't want to be one of those people that push and push and push against life. Always struggling. Never happy. I was happy the way I was. Yes, I killed a man, and that's terrible. But it was an accident. You saw how fast I was driving that night. I was out of my mind. It was all Jenny's fault. She was always pushing at me, just like you. Never satisfied. Always disappointed in me. I couldn't take it anymore. I had to do it. In a weird way I think she'd be proud of me for finally showing some gumption. Too bad I'll never get the chance to ask her."

Ray swung his flashlight toward the other side of the shaft, illuminating a ruffled pink skirt and an expensive cashmere sweater. The beam crept up the crumpled body, revealing an arm from which protruded a jagged, broken bone. Was that what they called a femur, he wondered. Or was that in your leg? Didn't matter. She was dead. Almost three weeks now and she was bloating badly. Especially her face. He could hardly recognize her anymore.

"You should have known her when she was alive. Jenny really was very beautiful."

He swung the light back to Veronica again and even though she was clearly paralyzed he could have sworn she was trying to scream.

THE FAMILY PLOT

Sarah Bresniker

It was the flash of color among the headstones that caught my eye. I only ran through the old Pacific Grove cemetery when the coastal trail was overwhelmed with tourists. It was scruffy and rundown, but peaceful. There were more weeds than flowers, and even the weeds didn't get enough water to stay green for long.

The bright blue was a dress, worn by a woman lying on the dusty top of a grave, motionless. I veered off the path and ran toward her. As I approached, she popped up to a seated position and looked at me. When she moved, I screamed, and was immediately embarrassed.

"Oh!" she exclaimed. "Did I frighten you, hon? I didn't mean to!"

She had long gray braids and eyes that perfectly matched her dress. The dress was loose and flowing, and she wore practical sandals. She didn't look like a ghost, or a corpse, but rather like an aging flower child.

"Are you alright?" I asked, even though I was the one who had screamed.

"I'm good," she replied. "Sorry to frighten you. I just wanted to see how it will feel, when I'm dead." This was not the response I had expected. "This is my grave, reserved just for me. Weird, right? My whole family is here, nearly. My parents, my brother, cousins, aunts, uncles. It's almost like Thanksgiving, all of the relatives you try to avoid, right here in one place. Except that it's forever."

"I thought that maybe..."

"You thought I was dead. I can see that. But if I was dead, I'd be buried, right? Everyone else is buried, I'm pretty sure."

"I'm Arlie." I glanced at the headstone behind her. "I'm assuming you're...Elizabeth?"

"Izzie, please." She followed my eyes. The headstone read *Elizabeth Annabelle Waverly, January 13, 1949-*. "No one's called me Elizabeth for years. And now you know a few of my secrets. My real name, my age, my birthday. I expect a card next year!" She smiled. "If I make it that long." The smile faded. "Somebody wants me dead. That's why I thought I should see how it feels."

"Why would anyone want you dead?"

"Let's see. Money. Secrets. Jealousy. The usual stuff. Or maybe I'm just really annoying, to certain people."

Apparently, this woman led a complicated life. Or had a vivid imagination. Some people may have dismissed her and kept on running, but not me. Secrets? Jealousy? Murder? These were things I could never resist. "Someone may want you dead. But that's a long way from actually murdering you. Do you really believe you're in danger?"

"Well, yeah. Lately it feels like death is very close."

As she said this, I noticed that, unlike the other graves, one behind hers was mounded and freshly dug. I read the headstone and realized her mother had died only last week.

"I'm so sorry for your loss. If you really do think your life is in danger, you should come by the library."

She gave me a quizzical look. "Not the cops? What good would the library do? Do you have a big self-help section? Like how to solve your own murder?"

I was used to this response and told her about the unusual little library where I worked. For decades now, people have come from all over California, and farther, to visit the reference desk at the Pacific Grove Public Library. Thanks to the unique guidance and funding of the Society of Helpful, Resourceful, and Enquiring Women—known as SHREW for short—our mission has been to not just answer any question asked at our reference desk, but to solve problems. Even mysteries, even murders. Because of this, our skills go beyond those of ordinary public librarians. So, my interest in her story wasn't pure nosiness. It was part of my job. And also nosiness.

"I think I've heard something about that," she said. "And the police would probably think I'm an old loon. Thank you, Arlie, maybe I will come by."

With that, we said our goodbyes and I continued on my run, looking at the surrounding headstones, committing the names and dates to memory. I couldn't help but wonder who wanted her dead. We may be warned about stranger danger, but the true threat is usually much closer.

When I got to the library later that morning, my boss Nora called to me from her office. Although I've been working for her for a while now, I'm always impressed by the consistency of Nora's appearance. She is tall, at least six feet, and built like a retired sumo wrestler. Straight, light brown hair never strays from a chin-length bob. I think she trims it precisely an eighth of an inch each week, or she just wills it not to grow. She thinks more and moves less than anyone I've ever met. Even her gray-brown eyes move slowly, but she never misses anything going on around her.

"Arlie, what's on the calendar today?"

"The usual, but we may have an interesting reference question coming in," I responded, and told her about meeting Izzie in the cemetery, not bothering to mention the part where I screamed.

"Unless she comes in, it isn't our concern. You know the policy."

Yes, I knew the policy: *We're not busybodies*, Nora likes to say. *We're librarians.* We only provide information when asked. Nora takes our mission seriously, but she doesn't go looking for work. She'd rather spend her time reading or researching recipes for her wife Mitzie to make, than taking on difficult questions. Mitzie is one of the best chefs on the Monterey Peninsula. Nora is her best customer *and* her harshest critic. Arguing over food is their love language.

I sighed in frustration as I unlocked the front doors. I was immediately busy, but kept one eye on those doors, hoping Izzie would walk in. Unlike Nora, I thrive on action and the thrill of a real mystery. After all, the first books I ever checked out from the library were Nancy Drews. Not everyone gets into the library business to shush people.

Before long, someone came in who wasn't Izzie, but who did catch my eye. The first thing I noticed were her boots: thigh-high, red leather stilettos. She walked in those boots like she was born in them. Her blonde hair was teased and long, and a fringed, black leather jacket completed the look. As she approached my desk, I realized she had to be at least sixty, and my appreciation for her balance grew.

"Are you a librarian?" she asked me. "One of those ones who answer whatever questions I ask?"

"That's me. What can I help you with?" I was hoping she didn't just want directions to the restrooms.

"My sister, she has something that belongs to me. She says she doesn't have it, but I know she does. How do I make her give it to me? The police are no good—they said I should talk to you. I wanted them to file an injection or something, but they said I need proof. How can I show them proof when she's hiding everything?"

Thank you, PGPD. We have, let's call it, a complicated relationship with the local police force. On one hand, we've assisted them with some major cases, and we rarely take credit publicly. On the other, we've also pointed out their errors, or, as Inspector Chu would say, "caused difficulties" when they have rushed to judgment. As a sign of appreciation, the officers like to refer the so-called "nut jobs" to the friendly librarians at the Pacific Grove Public Library. They think they're punishing us, but honestly, some of my favorite people are "nut jobs."

"What is it your sister took from you, ma'am?" I asked.

"Ma'am? My name is Stevie," she said with a huff. "My family's treasure. My sister took it and half of it is mine."

"Okay, where did she take this treasure from?"

"If I knew that, I would have gotten it before her! You're not going to be any help!" She tossed her head in frustration at my lack of customer service.

Just then, Izzie stomped in, no longer looking so mellow.

"Stevie!" she shouted. Heads popped up from books and computers throughout the library. "What are you doing here?"

Izzie was the sister? She hadn't mentioned treasure. And what happened to that laid-back old hippie I met earlier?

"I'm here to find the treasure you stole!" Stevie yelled back.

Izzie kept stomping until she was directly in front of Stevie. "I stole? You stole!" Neither of them was using their library voice, and everyone around us was paying attention now, hoping for some free entertainment.

"Ladies," I said, "I need you to quiet down. If you can't be civil you will have to leave."

Izzie took her voice down a notch. "This is who I was telling you about this morning. The one who's trying to kill me!"

Everyone was glued to the drama now. While I was contemplating my response, Nora appeared behind me. "Perhaps this is a conversation better continued in my office." Her utter stillness and low tone had an immediate effect on both women, and they obediently followed her.

Once there, I took my usual seat in the corner. The two women sat and glared at each other while Nora made her way behind her desk. Despite their different appearances, once I saw them next to each other, it was clear they were sisters. Under all of the eyeliner and the giant hair, Stevie had the same blue eyes as Izzie, and the shape of their noses was identical, and somehow familiar.

"Nora," I began, as I sat down. "Meet Izzie and Stephanie Anastasia Waverly."

Stevie's glare moved to me. "I told you my name is Stevie! And I definitely didn't tell you my middle name. No one gets to use that!"

"I saw it on your tombstone."

The blood drained from her face. She looked confused for a moment, then sighed. "That was my mother's idea. As soon as anyone was born, she planted their headstone in the family plot. Her way of keeping us tied to Pacific Grove, I guess. Although it didn't work. We got out of here as fast as we could. Well, except Jerry."

"Your brother?" I asked. I remembered the name from the cemetery. "He died in the nineties, didn't he?"

"Yes," Izzie replied. "Who knows why, but he stayed around to take care of Mom long after we got out. Then he died in a car accident. He was so young." Both sisters drooped at the mention of their brother's death.

"Izzie, this morning you told Arlie you feared for your life. Is Stevie the person you're afraid of?" Nora asked.

Izzie's eyes slid toward Stevie. "Of course. Who else would want to kill me?"

"You would be a better judge of that than I," Nora replied.

Izzie's hands clenched. "I don't have enemies!" she protested. "Not around here..."

"And Stevie," Nora said, "what makes you think Izzie has some kind of treasure?"

"Because I've looked everywhere in Mother's house. After Jerry died, Mother never stopped talking about 'the family treasure.' Izzie got here before I did, so if it's gone, she has to have it."

"Are you both staying at the house now?" They nodded at Nora. "Arlie, why don't you accompany these two lovely ladies back home? With their permission, perhaps you can look around to see if you can come to any conclusions about the treasure. If we can solve that mystery, no one will have to murder anyone."

The "lovely ladies" glowered at each other before responding.

"I did ask for your help," Stevie said.

"I'd feel safer having someone else around," Izzie agreed.

The house was big for Pacific Grove, two stories with a front porch, probably built in the early 1900s. Izzie popped up the stairs to unlock the front door and Stevie pushed her aside to get through first. Inside was chaos. Books had been rifled through and tossed on the floor. Plates were shattered, and clothes were scattered. I stepped in and slipped on a pile of what turned out to be catalogs from the 1990s. I fell backward and hit the door with my elbow before landing on my butt. Neither sister paid me any attention, so I scrambled back up, my elbow zinging with pain but my pride intact.

I waded through the rubble, taking pictures with my phone as I went, and sending them to Nora. I had no idea what she thought I should be looking for, or how being here would help. Upstairs, bookcases lined the hallway, which led to three bedrooms and a bathroom. The shelves were empty, and books, knickknacks, and torn papers littered the floor. I took more pictures, still not sure what mattered. Suddenly, I heard shouting from below and picked my way down to see what was going on.

In the living room, Stevie held a figurine of a parrot over her head, and Izzie was clawing for it.

"What is going on?" I yelled.

"The treasure could be in here," Stevie said as Izzie grabbed her arm. The parrot crashed to the floor, shattering into pieces, nothing but air inside.

"If there is any treasure here," I said, "you two have probably destroyed it without even realizing it."

They both stopped, looking around as though seeing what they had done for the first time.

"Stevie, do you really think that Izzie has the treasure? Do you think she'd still be here if she did?"

Stevie looked at Izzie. "Probably not. But I'm not leaving it all for her. Half of it's mine."

"And Izzie, do you really think that Stevie is trying to kill you?"

"She threw a paperweight at me! And she poisoned my coffee yesterday. I threw up right after I drank it."

"I missed you, didn't I? And you used that cream that had been in the refrigerator for ages. It's not worth it for me to kill you." Stevie slumped for a moment, then tensed again. "Unless you stole the treasure."

I sighed and called on the conflict resolution skills I'd learned teaching toddler story time. "Tell me what you can about this treasure."

Izzie spoke first. "It began after Jerry died. Our mother started saying we needed to come back and help her find the family treasure. We both left home early, right after our dad died, and rarely came home. At first, I thought she was talking about all the money our dad lost when his business went under, but she said, no, that meant nothing. So much more had been lost." She twisted her skirt in her hand, looking at the floor. "Most of the time, she was drunk. She said a lot of nonsense."

"Even when we were little, she was crazy," Izzie went on. "But for a while it was fun crazy. On holidays, all kinds of amazing treats would magically appear, and we could never find her hiding spot. She said she had a secret place where she hid her treasures. But I don't know. Maybe we were just kids and weren't as good at treasure hunting as we thought."

"It was real!" Stevie argued. "I looked everywhere. I never found a single Christmas present or Easter egg. She had a secret place. I know it."

It seemed pretty clear to me that there was no treasure, but I kept that to myself. "I'm going back to talk to Nora. Maybe she'll have some thoughts. Try not to do any more damage for now."

* * *

Nora had gone home for lunch when I got back to the library, and I knew better than to disturb her at mealtime. As I ate my own apple and yogurt, I thought about what I'd seen. Could there be a treasure? If so, what was it? Or did those two just need something to fight about?

When she returned, Nora had a large roll of papers under her arm. "I stopped by the Historical Society on my way back. They had some information on the Waverly family. Apparently, they're a colorful bunch. I think you'll find them interesting.

"Robert Waverly settled here after World War Two. He married Beverly Smith, a local girl, and they moved into the house you just visited. They were high society for a while, throwing money around, but then in the sixties, things went south, and his business partners turned against him. He'd been moving money around, skating by on pure charm. He was handsome, too." She turned her phone toward me. On it was a black and white wedding photo of a glamorous couple, he in his Navy dress uniform, she in a white lace-covered dress.

"They lost nearly everything, and not long after that a heart attack killed him. Beverly was able to hang onto the house, but not much else, and she became a recluse. Her son Jerry was the only one who stood by her. He was a quiet guy. He apparently worked here, at the library, for years, part-time."

"What about Izzie and Stevie?"

"Izzie had gone to San Francisco by then, into the hippie scene. Stevie was still in high school—she left home right before graduation. She went to L.A., and almost made it big in the seventies with some hair band, but they started fighting as soon as they made a bit of money and broke up."

This all matched up with what the sisters had told me, but I couldn't see how it helped with finding the treasure or knowing if it existed.

"The archivist also gave me these." Nora unrolled the papers onto her desk. "They have blueprints for many of the older buildings in town, including the Waverly house."

I bent over the blueprints and remembered walking through the rooms that morning. The main floor matched my memory. I turned that sheet over to view the layout of the second floor. Instead of a bookcase at the top of the stairs, there was a door. Four bedrooms and one bathroom. I knew there had only been three. And a large built-in bookcase at the top of the stairs.

"That's not right. There was no room at the top of the stairs." I knew I remembered it correctly and pulled up the pictures on my phone. The bookcase went from floor to ceiling and looked immovable. Or was it? As I zoomed in on one of the photos, Nora leaned over my shoulder and pointed to a faint line on one of the shelves, about six inches from the corner. A crack caused by the sisters? Or something else?

"I think you need to take another look," Nora said.

But first, I had a roomful of toddlers waiting for Miss Arlie's story time. I raced through the stories and songs, my mind on the treasure, then bolted for the Waverly house. When I reached their block, I saw lights flashing and a crowd gathering. What had happened? Had Stevie actually killed Izzie?

Inspector Chu stood at the edge of the yard with two uniformed officers. She wore her usual pink Burberry trench coat, her long dark hair pulled into a perfect chignon at the back of her neck. She was always the best-dressed person at any crime scene, and I was still wearing my Very Hungry Caterpillar T-shirt. White tents were lined up from the front porch to the street, hiding whatever was happening from curious neighbors.

"Hello, Arlie." She seemed both unsurprised and unhappy to see me. "Can you tell me how it is that you appear to be the last person to see the decedents alive? What were you all up to?"

Decedents? Were both Izzie and Stevie dead? Maybe it was a burglary? Had I missed something of value? Why had I left them alone? And how did Chu know I'd been here? "What happened?" I tried to mirror Inspector Chu's calm demeanor, but knew I'd failed.

"That's what we're trying to figure out," Chu said. "Apparently, someone ordered a food delivery. When the driver got here, no one answered. He was about to leave when he looked in the front window and saw the mess. He was afraid there had been a burglary. Both Ms. Waverlys were already deceased by the time officers arrived and got into the house. You were recorded on the doorbell camera across the street going in and out. I don't know what has been going on here, but I'm not surprised you and Nora are involved."

"Since you have me on video," I said, ignoring her jabs, "you'll know I left when both women were still alive. They walked me out to the front porch."

"True. That's why I don't suspect you of murder. But you do know more than you're telling me."

"I'm happy to share." Grateful for anxious neighbors, I explained about Mrs. Waverly dying recently, the feud, and the search for treasure that the sisters had been obsessing over since they got here.

"And do you think there is something valuable in the house? That someone else was after?"

"I didn't see anything, but it's hard to tell." As I said this, Chu turned her back to me and took a call. Rude.

An ambulance pulled away from the street as she faced me again. "Forensics is done, and the victims have been removed. Don't go anywhere, I will want to speak to you again."

"I could help. I have pictures of how it looked here this morning." I didn't mention that I was also dying to look at that bookcase. "If I go with you, we can compare."

Chu crossed her arms. "I suppose it would be faster. And I know that you know your way around a crime scene. Follow me. Don't touch anything, or you're out."

We put on those little booties and went through the tents into the house. Tape outlines of two bodies were at the bottom of the stairs. The air in the house was still and lifeless. What had happened here? Both Izzie and Stevie had their faults, but one thing they'd been was full of life. How could that change so quickly? And why?

I opened the photos on my phone, and Chu studied one of the entry. "All of this mess was here this morning?"

"Yes, they were both looking for the treasure, tearing everything apart. Oh wait!" I looked from my phone to the stairway. "That wasn't there."

I pointed to two pieces of white, lacy fabric strewn over the railing. Chu picked one up with a gloved hand.

"That's their mother's wedding dress." I recognized it from the picture Nora had shown me.

"Thank you, Arlie. That's helpful."

"Do you have a murder weapon?" I dared to ask, since she seemed pleased.

She paused. "Results are still preliminary, but they weren't shot or stabbed. Just blunt force trauma."

I moved toward the stairs. There were scuffs and brown marks on the wall that I thought were new.

"What are you doing?" Chu asked.

"I have more pictures of upstairs." I wanted to see that bookcase. As I got to the top, I saw it was gone. Nora was right. It had been pushed back, opening to a room that hadn't been there before. I scrambled in before Chu could stop me. The new room contained even more bookcases and had already been torn apart.

"This was their mother's secret place," I marveled. Nora knew. And somehow, Izzie and Stevie had figured it out, too. "When I was here this morning, this bookcase was just a bookcase." I showed Chu my photo.

She gingerly touched the bookcase/door. It couldn't swing closed because of the wreckage on the floor, but you could see the latch, and how pressing down on a portion of one shelf would release it. I wondered if it had been Izzie or Stevie who discovered it.

Curious about the books and papers littering the floor, I bent down to look closer. Chu scolded me. "Don't touch anything!"

"I'm not!" I held my hands up. What looked like a birth certificate had caught my eye. I squatted lower, hands still up. The name on the certificate was "Scarlett O'Hara Waverly," and the birthdate was the same as mine. My knees went wobbly, but I kept my balance, barely, my yoga practice paying off. I lowered the hand holding my phone to snap a picture.

Of course, Chu noticed. "What are you doing?" Since she was allowed, she picked up the papers I had photographed and looked through them. "What's the big deal, Arlie? It's just legal stuff."

I stood up and felt the blood rush from my head. I leaned against the wall and closed my eyes. Of all the people I had to confess this to, why her? "My birth name is Scarlett. And that's my birthdate. I'm adopted. I've never known anything about my birth family."

"So, you're telling me *you're* Scarlett O'Hara Waverly?"

"No, I'm Arlie Wynne. But maybe also, yes? I never knew my full birth name."

I slid down the wall, my butt hitting the floor with a thump, right on the bruise from this morning.

"Arlie, you need to get out of here. Now. I'll have someone take you home."

"But—"

"No but. You were the last person to see these women alive, and now it turns out you may benefit from their deaths. Out. What was I thinking letting you up here?" She shook the papers in frustration as I stood up.

Outside, she asked one of the uniformed officers to take me home. Once she left, I told him I'd rather walk and started back to the library. The fresh ocean breeze helped me think.

When I saw Nora, I could tell by the way she looked at me that Chu had called her. I plopped into a chair in front of her desk, feeling like a client instead of a librarian or a detective.

"Scarlett?" she asked, with the slightest hint of a smile. "You've managed to keep that a secret, even from me."

"I'll take that as a compliment." Nothing today was normal, not even Nora. "It's not my legal name. My parents were only told my first name and that my birth mother died. They knew Scarlett didn't fit me, but it's how they came up with Arlie. Now I know a lot more, I guess. But they're all gone."

"I'm sorry this is how you had to learn about your birth family." Nora's phone buzzed and she glanced at it. "Inspector Chu is here. Should I let her in?"

I thought a moment. "As long as she's not going to arrest me for murder."

"Just let her try."

A moment later, Inspector Chu knocked, then sat down in the chair next to me. "It's been quite a day," she said. Nora and I nodded. "You should have let us know that Izzie and Stevie had an altercation in the library."

"According to Stevie, it was one of your officers who sent her to us," I responded. "Have you figured out who killed them?"

Chu grimaced but didn't engage. Nora spoke instead. "Inspector Chu, do you have the forensic results back yet? It's still early, but I'm sure you suspect what they will tell you."

"I don't conclude anything until I have evidence." Chu's tone was sharp.

"It seems to me you have plenty of evidence, and I assume the forensics will only confirm what you already know. There was no murderer in that house, certainly not Arlie."

"You don't know that."

"I know very little time passed between the time Arlie left and the women died. I know that somehow, one of them finally opened the door to the secret room. I know they nearly came to blows over knickknacks, so I can only imagine how they acted when they found that room. At the top of a dangerous staircase. Given that they were both found at the bottom of that staircase, along with the shreds of what we know is their mother's wedding dress, I'm assuming they fought over it and fell when it ripped, likely fighting the whole way down."

I looked at Nora and knew that she was right. Chu said nothing. The only two living biological relatives I had, and they were both gone before I even realized it.

"I also know," Nora continued, "that Arlie's nose is identical to Izzie's and Stevie's. The overall family resemblance, in fact, is remarkable."

Nora suspected the truth, even before I found the birth certificate? Like I said, she notices everything.

The next morning, I ran through the cemetery again. When I got to the Waverly plot, I stopped. Only twenty-four hours earlier, I had seen Izzie for the first time. Soon she and Stevie would be here permanently, their mom winning at last. As I passed the foot of Jerry's grave—my father's grave—my foot caught in a hole. The plot was overgrown and weedy, the ground rough and dry, but the inside of the hole felt smooth. I cleared the weeds away and uncovered a flat stone. Not a headstone like the others, just a rectangle, more like a paving stone. As I wiped away the dirt, I could feel letters carved into it. "SOW" was the first line, "August 12, 1990-" the second. Scarlett O'Hara Waverly. It was mine. A shiver ran down my spine. I could be buried right here someday, if I wanted. With my con-artist grandfather, my depressive grandmother, my aunts who let nothing short of death keep them from what they wanted, and the biological father I never knew.

Or not. I didn't intend to need it for a very long time.

YOUR 10th BOND IS FREE!

Wendall Thomas

P.T. Barnum had nothing on my dad.

Of course, our suckers were specialized, but my father's belief that there was "a felon born every minute" kept us in Cheerios and chicken pot pies for my entire childhood. It had also supplied the mortgage on our bungalow with the arched doorways, fake fireplace, non-working heating vents, and built-in kitchen table, where I currently sat with my face buried in the fedora Bogie wore in *The Big Sleep*. It smelled like Brylcreem, Lucky Strikes, and old dollar bills.

My dad was wearing it when he was killed by a speeding Mustang GT at the intersection of Wilcox and Fountain a year ago. Today.

Ted, the Desk Sergeant on duty at Hollywood Station—and my former babysitter—arrived at the house with the hat. It told me everything I needed to know. It was one of the few things of Dad's I hadn't had to pawn, and right now, I couldn't seem to let go of it.

I poured a shot of Maker's Mark, remembering the day he found the hat with "Bogart, H." sewn inside the brim on our annual, pre-Halloween shopping spree. It was the fall of 1970. I'd been nine. Some dads took their kids to Sears; mine took me to the Western Costume warehouse sale.

"What's the point of living in Hollywood if you don't do

stuff like this?" he'd said, as he sprinted away to fight with Bea Arthur's stand-in over a Toreador outfit from *The Sun Also Rises*. The company had made costumes for the studios forever and as far as my dad was concerned, any place that sold the real sandals from *Spartacus* deserved repeat business. I missed him like crazy. But part of me was glad he wasn't here to see the sorry state his beloved bail bonds company was in.

I was tempted to have another shot and checked the clock—8 a.m. Better not. I smashed a couple of ice cubes on my eyelids, then donned a black fifties chiffon dress, my Chuck Taylors, a jean jacket, and Dad's hat, and squinted my way up Wilcox to the office. It was June and the air had that glary, yellowish tinge you got through cheap Rexall sunglasses.

I unlocked our three deadbolts and jerked the combination lock open. The iron bars rattled. I needed to tighten them again, but it would have to wait—the phone was already ringing. I hung Dad's hat on the coat rack, turned KRTH 101 on low, and reached for our greasy black phone.

"As You Were Bail Bonds. This is Ava."

I didn't add Ava with a hangover, fifteen extra pounds, three bail skippers, and a high interest loan due at the end of the day. I knew whoever it was wouldn't care. There was no greater narcissist than the newly arrested.

"Yeah, it's Slappy Adams."

"Hi, Slappy." Anthony "Slappy" Adams, fifty-two, had a weakness for opportunistic B&Es and high-end purse-snatching. Despite that, he was always broke, and sometimes did the odd job for us in exchange for bail money. This arrest and bond would put his punch card at a danger level of eight.

"Recidivism is everything," my dad used to say, after he'd had a couple of beers. His words got longer, rather than shorter, when he drank. That's when he would whip out some of his favorites, like "titular," "aggregate," or "insofar as." His vocabulary often got an eyeroll from the bouncers at Boardner's—the ones he hadn't bailed out, anyway.

Slappy coughed. "I'm across the street."

"What do you need this time?"

"The regular twenty-five grand. It's all just, you know..."

"A misunderstanding. Right. I'm with a customer," I lied. "I'll be over in a bit." *Damn you, Harry Chapin,* I thought, as I clicked off the radio. It was the wrong day for "Cat's in the Cradle" to be on an hourly loop. I needed to pull myself together before I walked into the station. Nobody liked a sobbing bonds girl.

I was applying some restorative lip gloss when I saw a detective headed my way. He wasn't one I knew, but they all had what I call "the walk." They led with their shins. The iron bars jangled again as he crossed the four feet to our counter.

"Ava Jean Hansen?"

"The same. In need of a bond, Detective?"

"Not today. I just wondered whether this was one of yours?"

He held out an evidence bag with a business card that read, "Your 10th Bond is Free!"

I stared down at my showman father's greatest marketing achievement, a promise aimed directly at his favorite kind of clients, repeat offenders.

Our business model depended on aspirational, incompetent criminals accused of crimes with a bail amount under twenty-five grand. We got less up front, but we owed less if they disappeared. My father had this down to a science. He was partial to Bribery of a Public Official (who wasn't?), Campaign Violations, Assault with Deadly Weapon Other Than a Firearm, Indecent Exposure (within limits), Forgery, and Looting. In addition, Dad always went for an "Accessory" charge, since those clients were never the brains of an operation and could rarely organize a successful disappearance.

I took the card. The cartoon logo of a Harvey Pekar-esque figure jumping up and down was definitely ours. We had taken the "one punch per bond" idea from the Subway sandwich model, except our holes had to be initialed to count. I held the card closer and saw AJH over nine punched holes. Only the tenth hole, the one my jokester dad placed right over "Harvey's" crotch, was still intact.

"It looks like it. Where did you get it?"

"Are there many of these around?"

I pointed to the stack on the counter. "Thousands, probably."

"And how many offenders get to ten?"

I hesitated for a minute. The truth was I knew exactly how many, and also how many were at nine. I had to. Thankfully, right now, there was only one criminal with nine bonds who wasn't in jail. Uncle Curtis. What had he done now?

"Maybe twenty, over the years. Where did you get it?"

"In a homicide victim's pocket."

"Oh my God." I backed away and lowered myself into my chair. When you specialized in repeat offenders, all your clients felt like extended family. I didn't need to lose anyone else. Not today. "Who?"

"Someone named Trent Blankenship. Is he one of yours?"

I breathed a sigh of relief. I'd never heard of him. "Is it an alias?"

"He also goes by Trinny Dunedin, but Blankenship's the name that came up for the prints. He was a multiple offender. You never posted bail for him?"

"The names aren't familiar, but I'll check both."

I unlocked our filing cabinet and poked through. Had Dad kept files I didn't know about? Maybe. But either way, in this case we'd dodged a 10th-bond bullet, even if Trent Blankenship hadn't.

"Nope. Nothing."

I waited for the detective to leave. He didn't.

"How about Curtis Small?"

Oh no. "Curtis Small? What does he have to do with this?"

"His prints were on the card."

Shit. Uncle Curtis had been my father's best friend. Like most people, Dad met his friends through work. Curtis was one of a few clients who had been to our house and I knew him well, although, as a teen-aged girl, there was such a thing as having too many "uncles." Especially when you wound up having to do skip tracing on them.

"Are you sure it's a homicide?"

"Yes." He leaned over the counter. "Is he one of yours?"

"I believe so, yes. Let me check." I took my time rummaging through the files while I tried to manage my face. Being at danger level nine, Uncle Curtis's file was close to the top.

I looked up, as casually as I could. "Yeah, he is. The last time he was in was July, for a DUI. Fifteen hundred. He showed up in court. Why?"

"Can I see that?"

"Did you bring a warrant?"

"Seriously?"

"Parolees are entitled to privacy, too."

"Your files include private information that wouldn't be on file with us?"

"Possibly."

Absolutely. Our info included girlfriends, ex-wives, escorts, favorite bars, kinds of cars they liked to steal, their favorite movie theaters, bookstores, and newsstands, whether they preferred Hollywood Park to Santa Anita, burgers to burritos, Norm's to Ships. We had more alarming personal information about their sexual behavior, too.

"It's the principle," I said, closing the file and replacing it. In my backpack.

"Okay, well, where were you last night?"

"Me? You can't be serious." His face said he was. "I was home."

"Can anyone vouch for that?"

"Not unless parakeets can talk."

"You don't look like the parakeet type."

"Really? And what would that be?"

"Ugly-ish."

"Wow. I'm speechless for so many reasons."

"That's too bad, because I need to bring you in for questioning."

"Why on earth do you have to bring me in?"

"There was another set of prints on the card. Yours."

Unfortunately, all bondspeople had their prints on file.

"Of course they are. I gave it to him, or whomever, and I initialed it. My prints are on all our cards."

"I still need to bring you in."

"I can't just leave."

"Sure you can. Lock up, you'll be back in half an hour. Hour tops."

"What's your name, anyway?"

"Galvin. I usually work downtown." He handed me his card.

At least I could post bail for Slappy while I was there. "Just a second." In the guise of finishing my lip gloss, I put some Vick's vapor rub under my nose. Hollywood Division gave the morgue a run for its money in the fresh-air department.

I locked up again.

"Normally I'd offer to send a squad car to pick you up, but all things considered," he said, as he offered his elbow and stopped traffic while we walked across the street. I guess that qualified as gallantry, for a cop.

We got a few nods and a lot of stares when we came through the Hollywood Station door. Pretty much everyone there had known me since I was a kid.

Ted looked up from the front desk. "Hey, Ava. Darlene said she saw you at Jazzercise." I had started with Jane Fonda classes. That hadn't worked, but since I'd bought the leg warmers, I'd moved on to the next exercise craze. To be honest, that wasn't working, either. It just made me want three Oki dogs instead of two.

"She's really good on the high kicks," I said.

Galvin cleared his throat, then gestured me down the hall.

"Come on. I have a hitman I want you to meet."

"We don't do bail for murder charges. We can't afford it."

"Good to know." He opened the door to a room that used to hold ten-pound bags of Folgers, bullet-proof vests, and unassigned handcuffs. Now it was filled with a humming, cement-colored machine the size of a walk-in closet.

"What the hell is that?"

"HITMAN. The Homicide Information Tracking Management Automation Network."

"Cute. What the hell does it do?"

"It's the newest thing in law enforcement technology. We're one of the first departments in the country to have it. It has a program that compiles all the aspects of the homicides, countrywide, in our files. It's going to cut our need for manpower in half. You can ask it ninety-eight questions about each death."

"Ninety-eight? You couldn't come up with two more?"

He frowned at me. "Ninety-eight is plenty. It identifies repeat offenders with just ninety-five, but we went the extra mile. It can locate cases by murder weapon, color of the getaway car, the nationality of the victim, the street where it happened. If there's a rash of murders involving an Uzi—a 9-millimeter machine gun-type weapon—we can figure it out instantly."

"I know what an Uzi is." I stared at the machine.

"I'm the only one in the LAPD who's trained to use it."

Men, I thought. "Any chance of a cup of coffee?"

"No." He reached for two folding chairs leaning on the wall and we squeezed in beside the humming monstrosity. Galvin patted the machine. "Anyway, this baby is how we found Curtis Small and that's why you're here."

"You don't seriously think Curtis Small killed this Trent guy, just based on the card."

"I can't discuss an ongoing investigation."

"That's all you've been doing."

He glared at me. "Just out of curiosity, how much money do you lose when someone gets to ten bonds?"

"Depends on the crime. Could be as low as a thousand, or maybe as much as fifteen."

"Has anybody hit it?"

"Yes." Recently. That was why I was overdrawn at the Gilmore Bank and had that meeting with a loan shark at the end of the day.

"So, it's not great for you, is it?"

"Like I said, it depends. My dad thought the repeat business put us ahead overall, kind of like the lottery. Plus, there's fine print. Clients are disqualified for the offer if they've ever not shown up for their court date, so it tends to be the most responsible criminals who get there."

"And what if one of your responsible clients gets charged with a homicide on their tenth bond?"

"That's why we only handle small-time offenders." I shook my head. "You don't seriously think I would kill someone to avoid paying the bond?"

"You'd be amazed how little people will kill for. According to HITMAN, Trent Blankenship was a suspect in a homicide last week. Over a parking spot."

"I told you, he wasn't one of ours." Thank goodness.

"But Curtis Small is? That is his bail card, right?"

"Who knows? I guess. But he was just a customer, I didn't really know him." I got a flash of my dad and Uncle Curtis on our couch, smoking cigarillos and making dirty jokes about the Macy's Parade balloons.

"Well, according to the computer, he's also killed at least two other people over the last ten years. We have a warrant out for him as we speak."

"Uncle Curtis? No fricking way!"

He grinned. Dammit. I hung my head in defeat.

"I guess you do remember him, if he's your uncle."

"He's not my real uncle. I just call him that. Didn't you have aunts and uncles who weren't aunts or uncles? Anyway, your magic machine made a mistake."

"It doesn't make mistakes."

"But he's only been charged with low level stuff—drunk driving, shoplifting, identity theft. Nothing violent."

"Nothing violent that you know of. That just means he didn't get caught. And he wouldn't have, without HITMAN. So, you're saying you didn't know about these warrants?"

"How could I possibly know about them?"

"Well, you have clients, you have friends on the force, you hear lots, I'm sure, through the criminal grapevine."

"The criminal grapevine? Seriously? Is there a union for that?"

"You know what I mean. Any chance you're hiding him?"

"Are you insane? No. And anyway, Uncle Curtis might be a sleazebag in moments, but he's not a murderer. He used to come for Thanksgiving. He always brought congealed salad."

"You'd have thought the congealed salad would have been a clue. That stuff is disgusting."

"Not if you use real cream cheese."

"Any chance your father knew about the violent stuff?"

"I don't know, let's ask him. Oh no, he's dead. Actually, he's been dead for a year. Happy Anniversary to me."

He looked down. "Sorry. I forgot."

"Forgot? How did you even know?"

"Because, based on the nationwide evidence the machine's compiled, we think Curtis Small was driving the Mustang that killed him."

I grabbed the seat of the chair with both hands to steady myself from the sudden bitch slap of horror and grief for my dad. It couldn't be true.

"I think I'm going to be sick."

I made it down all three hallways to the ladies' room. It still smelled the way it did when I used to hide in the stalls as a kid—like Ban Roll On, Lysol, and Pink's hot dogs.

With no female officers on duty, it was still a great place to hide. When I finally came out, Ted from the front desk was waiting with a towel, a bottled water, and some Tic Tacs. "I know. It's a hard day," he said. "Slappy's been asking for you."

"I bet." I followed Ted to his desk, downed the water, and asked for another.

I decided the detective could wait and took care of Slappy before I returned to the LAPD version of HAL.

When I got back to the computer room, Galvin was bent over the machine with the concentration of an eleven-year-old Super Mario Brothers addict. I watched him punch four numbers into the keypad.

There was something heartening about knowing my family of criminals was up against a man whose password was "0000." Criminy, as my dad would say. The machine beeped and hummed louder.

Galvin still hadn't noticed me, so I tried to memorize everything he was doing. I'd write it all down when I got back to the office. Eventually, he hit a red button and papers started to shoot out of the machine's plastic jaws.

He turned to catch one and noticed me in the doorway. "Miss Hansen. Feeling better?"

"Ms. Not really. Are you going to charge me?"

"No. Just covering all the bases." He walked me out to the parking lot. "Don't go far."

"I live on Lexington. I pretty much operate in a three-block radius."

"Great, keep it that way."

"Look, Uncle Curtis has always driven a Caddy. He doesn't have a Mustang. We keep track of these things."

"Maybe he just doesn't have a Mustang you know about. Or his girlfriend does." He looked across the street at our blinking neon sign. "As You Were Bail Bonds," he read. "Where did that come from?"

"Aardvark, Awesome, and Abracadabra were taken. No, really, my dad did two tours in Vietnam. He started with veterans. He thought they would get the double entendre."

"I am sorry about your dad." He shook my hand and stood there until I'd gotten across the street.

As soon as I was back in the office, I wrote down all the steps and codes for HITMAN, tucked Ted's master key—snatched while he got me more water—in the safe, and took the important papers out of it. I put them in my backpack with Uncle Curtis's file. It was almost noon. I needed ten thousand dollars by five o'clock. I was counting on Slappy.

He appeared, right on time, bringing half of his bail fee and the names of three low-level felons he'd befriended overnight. The crimes were in the right price range, but they were unknowns, so it was still a risk if they jumped bail. Today, it was a risk I was willing to take. As Dad always said, "We'll worry about tomorrow three days from now."

I gave Slappy all his paperwork and asked if he'd watch the office for a couple of hours. He was always eager to work off his debt by helping out. I stopped by my favorite locksmith for a duplicate key, then headed back into the station and replaced Ted's original while he retrieved Slappy's friends. I managed to convince them that we were the best bail bonds deal in town and took their money. Five thousand dollars down. Five thousand more to go.

I was starving and needed time to think, so I headed to Miceli's. Too much garlic and tomato sauce always cleared my head. I raised a glass of my father's favorite cheap Chianti to his memory and thought about what he would do if he were here. Then I unzipped my backpack and got to work.

By the time I'd finished off my baked ziti and the files, it was one o'clock. Four hours left. I ran through a mental list of items in our house, but I'd pawned everything that was worth more than a hundred dollars. I'd already taken out a second mortgage on the office property and sold Dad's 1970 Ford Falcon, which had broken my heart.

Then I thought about Uncle Curtis. I didn't believe he'd murdered Trent Blankenship or anyone else. He was too lazy.

He would call a taxi to go a block. As a physical coward, he was peerless. And why would he hurt Dad? They were pals. My father had even left him five grand in his will. He was as close to family as it got. For us, anyway.

Still, guilty or not, if the LAPD found and charged him with a homicide, much less two, and he was on his tenth bond, As You Were would be on the hook for a hundred thousand dollars, minimum, and a million if he skipped out. I needed to find him before they did.

I bet he was still in L.A., and I knew he liked to lay low in comfort. When he was late for his last hearing, I'd found him in the jacuzzi at a Koreatown spa on Beverly.

There was a chance if I could find Curtis, he'd give me the five grand I needed in exchange for a heads-up about the warrants and enough time to get out of town. I drove to Beverly Hot Springs, just east of Western, where the non-rich and semi-rich, mostly female, exfoliated.

They said I'd missed him by half an hour. It was the first baked ziti I'd ever regretted.

I figured he'd gone for a late lunch. And if he'd actually killed someone, he'd want comfort food. He was partial to the soul food at Maurice's Snack 'n Chat on Pico, so I headed west.

I ran a couple of stop signs on the way to the restaurant, but once I got there, I just stood in the parking lot for a long time. Then I walked to the nearest pay phone and called Slappy.

I found Uncle Curtis tucking into some yams on the patio. His comb-over had gotten thinner. His beer gut hadn't.

"Ava! Hey, sweetie. Don't you look luscious today. You want anything?"

I sat down across from him and took the basket of biscuits he offered. I was stuffed, but I needed to buy some time. I managed to force down a piece of fried chicken too, then looked at my watch.

"You gotta be somewhere? Or you got time for dessert? Their cobbler is to die for."

"I'm just not that hungry. It's the anniversary of, you know...Dad."

"Oh. Right. Is it? I'm sorry, I forgot. Whatcha doin' here, anyway?"

I'd seen a lot of damsel-in-distress looks over the years, so I could mimic a first-rate one. "Uncle Curtis, I'm in a tight spot. I took out a loan to cover a bond and it's coming due today. I can't afford it, and I really can't afford the vig."

"Who with?"

I told him. He shook his head.

"He doesn't mess around. How short are you?"

"Not that much. Five grand."

He went pale. "He'd kill someone over five grand, easy. Sure you can't come up with it?"

"I've tried everything. You don't have any of the money from Dad's will, do you? Could you cover me, just for a week? I promise I'll pay you back. It's almost the Fourth of July; we always score big that weekend."

He looked at me for a long time, then nodded. "Sure, kiddo. For your dad's sake."

If he hadn't said that, I might have changed my mind.

He made a big show of pulling out his checkbook and writing the amount with a flourish. As I tucked the check into my backpack, I noticed the bastard hadn't signed it. No problem. I had been raised by a man who considered driving a stick shift, holding your liquor, and basic forgery as things every daughter should know.

Curtis left a single on the table and grabbed his leftovers. When we got to the parking lot, he froze for a second, then looked left and right. "What the hell?"

"What's wrong?"

"My damned car is gone."

"Your Mustang?"

The GT, with a dent on the front and no plates, had been parked in the lot when I arrived.

He went pale for the second time in five minutes.

"That's bad luck. Want a lift? Or should we call the cops to file a report?"

"No, don't worry about it. I'll figure it out."

"You're sure?"

He nodded.

"Okay. Good luck." I stood on tiptoes and gave him a kiss. I wondered how he'd felt, just before he ran over my father. I realized I didn't care.

I headed for my local Gilmore Bank branch at 3rd and Fairfax. I knew Gerry the cashier, another former babysitter, would cash the check for me.

Then I found another phone booth and pulled out Detective Galvin's card. When he heard that Uncle Curtis had been spotted at the Beverly Hot Springs, he said he was on his way.

I hurried to the station and told Ted I'd left my makeup bag in the bathroom. I unlocked the HITMAN closet, shut the door, and punched in 0000. It only took a minute to remove a few crucial details from a series of B&Es Slappy had admitted to and print out a list of repeat offenders we hadn't serviced yet.

By the time Galvin and his backup got to the spa, a hit and run had already been reported at Pico and Sierra Bonita. The driver had abandoned the Mustang GT and run. No witnesses. Curtis Small was dead at the scene, a Styrofoam box of peach cobbler splattered a few feet away.

I made my five o'clock meeting in the Musso and Frank's parking lot, paid off my loan, and headed back to the office.

When Slappy returned, I handed him a beer to celebrate. I let him know he was clear on the twenty-five hundred and also on some former B&Es, and he assured me he'd worn gloves and wiped down the car.

I figured having Curtis hit by the Mustang GT would, at the very least, freak HITMAN out and even better, invalidate its results. I liked the cops at the station. I didn't want them replaced by a soulless box.

Slappy put down his beer. "We still have our deal?"

"Absolutely."

He held out his "Get Out of Bail Free" card. I crossed out the "10th," replaced it with "9th" and initialed the change. After he left, I tightened the screws on our iron bars, then put all the papers back in the safe, grateful that Dad always made bailees take out a life insurance policy payable to As You Were Bail Bonds before he would process their release. Uncle Curtis's had been for a hundred grand.

Take that, suckers, I thought, as I grabbed my father's fedora. Nothing comes for free.

THE DEVIL LIKED BASEBALL

John Edward Mullen

I picked up my detective partner, Buddha, outside his two-story house in Mira Mesa. Our unmarked sedan listed to starboard as he dropped his weight onto the passenger seat.

"How was your vacation?" I asked.

He emitted a low growl through clamped lips. "I finished Nancy's honey-do list yesterday—just before dinner."

"That explains why I didn't see you at the Padres game yesterday afternoon."

Buddha's tiny, brown, x-ray eyes gave me the once over. "Jesus."

"What?" I said.

"You've got your Sir Lancelot look about you this morning: dark rings around the eyes, unshaven, and," he sniffed the air three times, wrinkling his nose like a rabbit, "you're wearing your favorite brand of cologne: Yesterday's Sweaty Shirt."

Buddha shook his head, wriggling his three chins. "You're still sleeping with that eighteen-year-old's mother, right? The one we met at the station two weeks ago, the blonde with the big, blue, doe eyes and enormous boobs."

"It's not what you're thinking. I'm on a mission."

"Right. A mission to hump every needy woman you meet."

"Alice is different."

"Her first name's different."

I pulled away from the curb. Buddha rolled down the passenger side window and lit one of his Al Capone cigarillos.

"Do you have to smoke in the car?" I said.

"I'm on a mission, too." He sucked noisily on his cigarillo, turned, and blew the smoke in my direction. "If I'm lucky, I'll die of lung cancer before you find yet another woman to save."

"It's not just Alice," I said. "There's her son, Billy, too. He needs a man in his life to help guide him. He has a chance to make something of himself if he can kick the drug habit. I just need to convince Alice to boot Neil—that's Billy's sleazebag friend—out of the house. Then she'll have a chance to turn her son around."

"How long has the sleazebag been staying with them?"

"Six months."

"Six months?" Buddha flicked ash out the window. "Don't you think if she wanted to kick him out, she'd have done it by now?"

"She'll do it. I just need a little more time to convince her."

Buddha rolled his eyes. "You must hold the record as the person who's been reincarnated more often than anyone else."

"I can't deal with mysterious this early in the morning. What do you mean?"

Buddha blew smoke in my face again. "They say there's a fool born every minute. You're him."

"Fuck you."

Buddha showed me the back of his fist, his way of flipping me the bird—his left hand is missing the middle finger.

"Actually, I'm with Frank Zappa on that one," he said. "The curse should be 'un-fuck you.' Now, point the car toward Starbucks, oh junior detective, unless of course, you feel the need to stop at the nearest Catholic church and confess your sins."

"Starbucks is fine."

"Good. We both need coffee and it's your turn to buy."

***

A week later I sat in bumper-to-bumper traffic on the freeway, crawling north to Encinitas where Alice lived. We were scheduled to go to dinner after dropping her son, Billy, at a Narcotics Anonymous meeting. I tapped my fingers on my steering wheel, accompanying the surf music classic "Pipeline," the high-energy version with Stevie Ray Vaughn sitting in with Dick Dale. Pipeline. Waves. A moist tube. Rhythms. Alice. I shook my head.

The slow traffic and Buddha's often-repeated comments had me thinking. I'm pushing forty, maybe I should settle down. Alice was so sexy and so vulnerable. The combination drove me crazy. I couldn't help myself. I was head over heels. And just thinking about the last three nights in bed with Alice gave me a hard-on. Maybe we could make it a quick dinner and still have time for sex.

I exited the freeway at Manchester, sped north to Encinitas Boulevard, and parked in the lot of Alice's apartment complex. My God-I'm-glad-to-see-you grin melted away as soon as the door opened.

Alice didn't open it. Neil-the-sleazebag did.

Neil took a thermometer out of his mouth. "I'm the only one here," he said. He checked the thermometer. "And I got a fever of a hundred and three."

He looked green. He put his hand to his mouth. His cheeks billowed and he bent over. I jumped out of the way as he vomited onto the door mat and down the front of his camouflage jacket.

"Must be the weed," he said. He was still bent over. "Billy got sick, too. His mom took him to the hospital." He spit a couple of times into the shrubs alongside the building. "You gotta take me to the hospital, man. I'm real sick. I think I might die."

I thought, *We should be so lucky.*

I said, "Clean yourself up, first."

He went to the kitchen and used paper towels to wipe most of the puke off his coat. Then we got in my car.

I had half a notion to take Neil out to the desert and dump him. Damn fool said he combined marijuana with water and mainlined it. He also told me that Billy had shot up the same mixture and Alice had taken him to Scripps Hospital just fifteen minutes earlier. If Billy died from the drugs and I left Neil in the desert, the coroner might put two and two together and come up with my badge number.

"See this," Neil said. He pointed at a puncture wound on the inside of his arm. The skin around it looked red and swollen. "That's where I shot up. It itches."

I had an itch, too, but couldn't scratch it. That would entail arresting this scumbag meth addict. But I couldn't. I hated the fact that Neil felt so sure he was safe from arrest. He knew it would upset Alice if I put him in jail.

As I drove, Neil rocked back and forth. He moaned. He asked me five times a minute if we were there yet. I should have been with Alice, not chauffeuring this loser to the hospital. I wanted to take the butt end of my 9-millimeter pistol and scrape the whining lips from Neil's pock-marked face. If he lost a few of his nicotine-yellowed teeth, so much the better. As we sped south on I-5, I fantasized where I could best position his molars and bicuspids amid the remaining scrambled-egg-and-bacon puke on his tattered camouflage jacket. I was so captivated by these thoughts that I had to cut off two horn-blaring cars to make it onto the off ramp at Santa Fe Drive.

I pulled up outside the entrance to the emergency room and Neil opened the passenger door. He began to slide out but stopped. He reached into a pocket of his camouflage jacket and pulled out a bottle of pills.

"This is my stash. Keep this for me and don't lose it. The hospital might confiscate it."

I about broke the gear lever as I jammed it into park. I grabbed the bottle out of Neil's hand and jumped out of the car. A dumpster sat around the corner from the ER's double doors. I sprinkled the pills around the crap in the dumpster.

"Hey, man," Neil whined, "that was mine."

I marched to within two feet of Neil and threw the bottle at his chest.

"I don't give a fuck. It's trash and now it's where it belongs." I pointed at the dumpster. "You want to join it? I can arrange that."

For the briefest instant, fear showed in Neil's eyes. He turned and took a step toward the ER. I grabbed his arm and spun him around.

"Listen to me, asshole," I said. "You can't share Billy's bedroom any longer. Understand? Assuming you live, I don't want to see you hanging around Alice's ever again. Pack up your shit and don't...come...back."

His half-closed gaze—part feigned innocence, part stupidity, and part overdosed pain—assessed my seriousness. All the while he knew the hold he had on Billy, and how he had parlayed that into a permanent berth in Alice's home. Wasn't my driving this gutter pus to the ER proof he had us all over a barrel?

Neil laughed as he shuffled off toward the ER entrance. "See ya."

Alice wouldn't take my calls for a couple of days after I told Neil he had to leave. I had made him feel *unwanted* and pissed Billy off. Billy was eight years younger than his leech of a friend. He was everything Neil wasn't: effortlessly popular and bright—but gullible. He measured his worth by helping the underdog, and Neil was the under-est mongrel I ever saw.

At good ol' Neil's suggestion, he and Billy decided to visit friends for a while. That meant they were couch-surfing and hanging out with other young addicts or dealers, unless they scored enough cash for a motel room by collecting a fee buying kegs for underage parties, or peddling drugs. Alice, patron saint of patience and enabling, wouldn't be able to keep an eye on Billy, or make sure he got fed, or drive him to his Narcotics Anonymous meetings. So I, not Neil—the one who held Billy down—was the bad guy. Funny, Neil always managed to twist the reality surrounding his sorry ass. I spent the next two weeks sleeping alone, sore at Neil.

Strike one.

For half a second, I thought about dumping Alice, but I was hooked. I've always been a sucker for a damsel in distress. Convincing Alice to kick Neil out of her apartment was proving more difficult than I expected. If she wouldn't kick him out, maybe I could figure a way to remove Neil from the picture, or from the planet.

At the shooting range, the silhouette targets took on Neil's lanky, hunched form. Each time I took aim, I daydreamed about how I might do him in without going to prison. Thinking about murdering a guy bothered me almost as much as Neil did. There had to be some way to make him disappear.

Neil was so different from Billy. Billy liked books and loved talking about big ideas: what he considered fair or just, why kids should have all the freedom they want, why drugs should be legal. I didn't often agree with him, but at least he thought about things.

Neil was a zero. He rarely contributed anything to a conversation. His typical utterances were grunts or complaints. Mostly he complained about anyone who competed with him for Billy's attention. According to Alice, every time Billy made a new friend—which he did daily—Neil spent all his energy trash-talking the new kid. Nobody was good enough to spend time with Billy, other than Neil. I laughed at the irony. Dirty, foul-mouthed Neil demanded that Billy's friends be like Boy Scouts—trustworthy, loyal, helpful, friendly, courteous, kind, and the rest. Everything Neil wasn't.

Neil was good at getting other people in trouble. Alice told me that Neil was the one who thought it would be easy for Billy to shoplift a bottle of vodka at the local supermarket. Billy got caught. Neil got off scot-free.

After fifteen days of silence, Alice called. "Billy's back. He's totally strung out, but he's alive and back home. My car's at the mechanic's. Could you give Billy a ride to an NA meeting and pick him up after?"

"Sure. No problem." I crossed my fingers. "Is Neil back?"

"Yes, but he doesn't want to go to the meeting."

A small blessing.

"I've missed you, Alice."

"I've missed you, too, Larry."

"How about us going to dinner some time, just the two of us?"

"Okay."

Hot damn. I was back in.

I picked Billy up late the next afternoon. Neil not going gave me an opportunity to ask Billy about his buddy. We drove west on Encinitas Boulevard and turned south onto Old Highway One. Half of an orange sun still hung above the Pacific Ocean.

"If Neil gets you in trouble, why hang with him?" I said. "What kind of a 'friend' is he really? Friends don't drag their friends down."

Billy's response was typical for him: "Friends don't dump friends just because they screw up sometimes."

I pulled into the parking lot of the church where the NA meeting was being held and parked. "I admire your sense of loyalty," I said, "but don't you think loyalty should be earned?"

"No. Try being nice to Neil for a change. He's had a hard life."

Billy sauntered toward the door to the church's meeting room. I sat in my car thinking about Neil's almost supernatural hold on Billy. My thinking seemed slow, probably because I was de-caffeinated. I drove to a burger joint and ordered two cups of coffee. I sat in the restaurant parking lot and guzzled both of them. After five minutes, I had a revelation.

Neil was a devil.

His only gift was his ability to bring out the worst in people. Especially the worst in Alice, who had just started talking to me again.

I needed a way to cement myself into Alice's good graces.

And into her bed. I remembered one time when I'd taken Alice to dinner, while Neil sat in the living room of the apartment transfixed by a Padres game on the TV. I got my second revelation of the night.

I went back to the church at eight p.m. to drive Billy home. He and a girl about his age strolled out of the meeting, holding hands. Billy walked her to her car and, as best I could make out in the dimly lit parking lot, they spent five minutes swallowing each other's tongues before she drove off. After Billy got in the car, I told him that I'd be willing to take him and Neil to a game at Petco Park.

"That's really cool. Thanks," Billy said. "Neil's a big fan. He'll like that."

As I had hoped, Alice liked the idea, too.

On game day, I drove to the apartment complex on Encinitas Boulevard. Alice opened the door. The matted gray carpet was stained in several new places near the two reclining chairs which sat on the opposite side of the living room from the TV. As usual, Billy sat in the blue chair and Neil in the fake leather one. Unlike other times I had dropped by, today a teenaged girl with dark hair streaked with purple dye sat on the arm of Billy's chair. She might have been the girl I saw Billy kissing at the church. One hand was draped around Billy's shoulders. Her other hand caressed Billy's cheek. Billy's neck bore the girl's territorial mark—a newly created hickey. Billy and the girl's eyes were locked. The two of them looked happy.

Neil didn't. He sat with his arms crossed. The brim of his Padres cap, pulled low, almost covered his eyes. He pretended to be absorbed in a television ad for a room deodorizer.

"Larry," Alice said, "this is Robin."

Robin hopped up and shook my hand. She was a little thin, but she had bumps in places Billy would appreciate. Her smile seemed to lift the depressing fog that usually took hold of the living room whenever Neil was there. A girlfriend might be just the thing to get Billy to dump Neil. I smiled.

When the introductions were over, Alice dragged me by the hand into the apartment's rear bedroom. After closing the door, she fell into my arms, trembling.

"I don't know what to do," she said. "Billy came home yesterday afternoon all upset. He'd shot up meth again and was really depressed. I reminded him that all addicts relapse and that he shouldn't feel defeated. I told him I'd borrow more money if he wanted to go back into rehab. He said he knew I couldn't afford it and he wouldn't let me get more in debt because of him."

I hugged her a bit tighter.

"It'll be okay," I said.

"You haven't heard it all. A little later, Robin called, and I heard Billy say that Neil had scored some more meth. Robin came right over and took Billy to an NA meeting. The two of them were out all night and I was left alone with Neil. He paced up and down in the living room talking crazy. Something was sticking out the back of his camouflage jacket, almost like he had a tail. I confronted him about the meth. He got angry and pulled a machete out from under his coat. He waved it in the air and shouted, 'Keep away, bitch!' I ran into my bedroom and locked the door."

I resisted the temptation to shake her. "Jesus, why didn't you call me? I could have arrested the bastard."

"You can't. Billy might run away again," Alice said. "I won't lose him like I lost my daughter. He's all I've got."

"Fuck."

I shook my head in a double-take effort to rattle some sense out of what was, to me, gross stupidity.

"Alice, for the thousandth time, you've got to throw Neil out of the house."

She wasn't listening. She had her own idea. Alice looked toward the door, and then whispered in my ear.

"Don't hit men use .22s? My father has a .22 rifle that's got to be seventy-five years old. It'd be untraceable, wouldn't it?"

I pushed her away from my shoulder and looked her in the eye.

"And what?" I whispered back. "You're going to pop Neil with it?"

"I thought, you know, when he was asleep, I could put the barrel against the back of his head."

"Jesus double-fucking Christ. Alice, you can't just go killing people. It's not like the cops won't figure out who had a motive, even if they can't find the rifle."

Her tear-filled eyes pleaded: *Help me. Help me save Billy.*

Neil shouted from the other side of the door, "I hope you're making it a quickie. We need to get going if we're going to get to the game on time."

"I'll think of something," I said.

I kissed her. She wiped tears from her face.

Talk about bringing out the worst in people. If I couldn't figure a way out of this mess, Neil the devil might turn Alice into a murderer.

Strike two.

As we entered Petco Park, I bought a program for the three of us to share. The two boys started arguing over who got to have the program, so I bought Neil his own to keep the peace.

I thought I'd done damn good, given the short notice, getting front-row seats in an upper box overlooking right field. I had to pay for the seats, plus promise to take a couple of weekend shifts for another detective who had season tickets. Neil wasn't satisfied.

"If the big dick detective wants to get in your mom's pants so bad, the least he could do is get seats behind home plate," Neil said to Billy.

I wanted to scream: How about under home plate? But I didn't have to, because for once, Billy took my side. "These seats aren't bad," he said. "Besides, you brought your glove. Here, you have a chance of catching a foul ball. Behind home plate, you'd have no chance."

A momentary quiet set in. Neil and Billy studied their programs. I prayed for patience. When the organ sounded, I got my hopes up. All three of us stood for "The Star-Spangled Banner."

When we sat down, Neil started a game in which he and Billy took turns punching the other's upper arm. I took some pleasure in the fact that it was Neil, not Billy, who called off the game. While he rubbed his sore arm, Neil asked if he could have a beer. I gave him some money and told him to get two. When he got back, Neil handed one of the beers to Billy.

"Nice try, but the second one's for me," I said as I took the cup out of Billy's hand.

Neil gave me a dirty look. "It's not like he's never had a drink, ya know."

"Not today," I said.

The Padres took the field against Milwaukee. The pitcher started well, striking out two of the Brewers in the first inning. The third out should have come on a high fly ball, but the center fielder apparently lost sight of it in the sun. The ball dropped just behind him.

In the bottom of the third, the Padres had the bases full and no outs. Billy and Neil and I were on our feet chanting along with everyone else in the stadium as the center fielder stepped up to the plate. The boys were into the game now. In Neil's case, his second beer may have helped.

The Padres were sure to score. More importantly, I was mending fences with Billy. He seemed to be enjoying himself, maybe happy to be out of his mother's sight. I'd even scored points by agreeing to talk to his mom about him getting a motorcycle after he'd been clean and sober for six months. And with any luck, Robin's presence in Billy's life would eliminate the need for drastic action against Neil. Everything was falling into place.

But I'd forgotten the Neil-effect. The center fielder ended the third inning by hitting into a triple play. In the fourth inning, with Brewers on first and third, the pitcher balked. How often does a pitcher balk, for Christ's sake? By the end of the fifth inning, Milwaukee was up by four. To top everything off, Neil had convinced Billy that Robin was cramping Billy's freedom. To show her what's what, Neil suggested that the two of them visit a whorehouse in Tijuana. I said very matter-of-factly that that might be a good place to get AIDS, and therefore risky. I kept myself from saying it would be stupid. Still, they weren't listening.

At the start of the sixth inning, the boys said they were hungry, so I gave Billy money for pizza and he and Neil took off for the concession stands. Billy came back with two slices of pepperoni pizza and handed me one. Neil held a beer in each hand. He made sure I saw that he was drinking from both cups before he took his seat. I hoped the beer would at least keep him quiet.

During the seventh inning stretch, Neil sang "Take Me Out to the Ball Game" loudly and out of tune. When his voice cracked on the lyric "I don't care if I never get back," I started praying, *God, could you please make that happen?* At this point, two middle-aged men each well over six feet tall and weighing 220 or better, came up to my seat. The big one had a Navy SEAL tattoo on his left bicep. The front of his shirt was wet from the shoulder down.

Mr. Tattoo asked, "Which one of you assholes has been spilling his beer over the wall?"

I looked at Neil. Billy looked at Neil. Mr. Tattoo followed suit. Neil snickered like he'd been caught stealing a cookie from the cookie jar.

"Come on outside, Giggles," Mr. Tattoo said to Neil. "We'd like to have a word."

I was sorely tempted to let Mr. Tattoo and his buddy do to Neil what I wanted to do to Neil. But if they beat Neil into a pulp, Billy might think it was my fault for not stopping it. I flashed Mr. Tattoo my shield.

"Here's twenty bucks," I said, "to get your shirt cleaned."

"That's kind of you, Detective, but I would prefer to kick his ass."

"Trust me; after I'm done, Neil will regret his stupid stunt."

Mr. Tattoo glared at Neil. "I'd like to stick around and watch," he said. "Maybe give you a few suggestions. But we want to leave early to avoid the stampede, so do me a favor, would ya? Don't leave him with more than one non-crushed testicle."

I smiled like I thought that was the best thing I'd ever heard. "Sure thing."

We shook on it. The bones in my hand felt the certainty that Mr. Tattoo's grip could have squeezed Neil's nuts down to pea-size.

"Billy," I said. "Trade seats with Neil. He and I need to have a little chat and I don't want to have to talk around you."

They switched seats. I counted to ten.

"Neil, your friends may think that your acting like an ass-hole is kind of cute. I don't."

"What's the big deal?" he said. "So, the dude got a little wet. So what?"

I put my arm around Neil's shoulders. He squirmed.

"I'll try to explain it in terms you might understand. Okay, sweetheart?"

I pinched his earlobe between my thumb and forefinger as hard as I could.

"Ow. Cut it out!" He tried to break my grip, but he didn't have the strength.

"You pull one more stunt tonight, and you walk the twenty miles back to Encinitas. Are we clear?"

"You're hurting me."

"Are you going to behave?"

"That's enough," Billy said.

"I'm not sure Neil understands."

"You made your point. Let him go."

I let go.

Neil lightly stroked his ear with his middle finger. "Ow, ow, ow. Man, I think he took a chunk out of it. I think it's bleeding."

"It's just a little red," Billy said. "Don't be a wimp."

"What are you picking on me for? Are you taking his side?"

"I'm not taking sides. Dude, you wasted beer."

"Oh."

We watched the top of the eighth inning in silence. The Brewers scored another run and went up by five.

In the bottom of the eighth, with two men on base, the Padres's first baseman smacked a fast ball in our direction, and we leapt to the short wall just in front of our seats, hoping to catch the ball. Neil stood on his precious commemorative program, which lay open on the concrete floor. He seemed a little wobbly. Maybe it was the beer. All three of us leaned out and stretched to meet the ball. Neil grabbed Billy's arm and pretended like he was going to pull him over the wall. As the foul ball dropped just out of our reach, Neil's feet slipped on the slick cover of the program he'd insisted I buy him. Both he and Billy might have fallen over the wall if I hadn't grabbed the backs of their shirts and pulled them back.

"Goddamn it!" I shouted. "You could have gotten Billy killed."

"I was just fuckin' around," Neil said.

"Leave him alone," Billy said. "Nothing happened."

Not yet. But I realized that it was only a matter of time before Neil did Billy some permanent harm, maybe even get Billy killed. I was not going to let that happen.

Strike three.

God, tell me, please, what can I do? At that moment, my eyes opened wide as inspiration sparked in my brain. My idea could work, but it would take a miracle. Still, I couldn't help grin at Neil.

"What?" he asked.

"Nothing."

Devils should know that eventually, God will smite them. On the next pitch, the first baseman hit a second high fly ball in our direction. What were the odds of that, one in a million?

Billy, Neil and I jumped up and reached out for the ball. Neil wobbled on his commemorative program once again. I placed my foot on the game program just behind Neil's feet. The ball headed right for us.

While I leaned over to try and catch the fly ball, my foot propelled the program backward. Neil's feet were torn out from under him. His upper body lurched forward. In the same instant that he caught the foul ball in his glove, Neil tumbled over the wall.

Billy tried to grab his friend, but the devil was beyond salvation. Neil's arms flailed as he fell twenty-five feet toward the empty seats below yelling, "Billy!"

At that point, I figured I had God's ear. As Neil flipped end over end, I prayed: *Our Father, who art in Heaven, let him land head first.*

An hour later, I spoke with Detective Angelina Rodriguez who headed up the investigation into Neil's death. Of course, I left out the part about my giving Neil an assist. And I made no mention of Neil being a devil. Rodriguez wrote it up as what I told her it was, just a tragic accident.

Billy was devastated at first, but his pain didn't seem to last. The next day when I went to the apartment to pick up Alice for our dinner date, Robin was there sharing the blue chair with Billy. He was laughing at something she said, and he had a new hickey on his neck.

The following day, I picked Buddha up in our unmarked sedan to begin our shift. He rolled down the window, lit up his Al Capone cigarillo, took a puff and exhaled. "So, what really happened to Neil?"

"Sometimes," I said, "prayers get answered."

THE ONE WHO WAS GOOD

Lynne Bronstein

Four girls, three stories. Transcribed from the Youth Correctional Officer's interviews:

LORI: You want to know how it happened? It happened because we were bored! We were off from school for the summer and had nothing to do. And that's all I'm going to say. Lock me up, what do I care?

DOREEN: It was Marla's idea. She gave us the assignments. They were nothing much at first. Like "I will lie," "I will steal something from my parents." Then it got worse. Marla was crazy. I never did like her that much. We were friends but I was scared of her.

JANIE: I don't know what to say.

I don't know what I did. But I'm sorry. Please believe me.

Please stop telling me that I know what I did. My parents are going to hate me forever for this. I want to go away and forget it all.

I can't tell you what I know. You won't understand.

I wanted to be popular. I wanted to be accepted. I thought Marla was okay. It bothered me when she made fun of me, but I figured I would just have to let her do that sometimes. But she was the worst. She wasn't good. I wish I had never met her.

***

LORI: I stuck with Marla because she was brilliant and fearless. She was the wildest girl I had ever met. She must have thought I was an airhead at first. A girl who was always doing her hair, putting on her lipstick. I guess I'm the glamour type. Marla was beyond definitions like that.

We both lived on the north side of Santa Monica, the canyon area where the richest people live. Her family was richer than mine. Their house had two stories, three if you counted the basement, and two wings. It had five bathrooms and a swimming pool. I loved that house. I loved Marla's hot pink bedroom and pink and white bathroom.

Hell, I loved Marla. She was the brunette and I'm blonde, but she was the really hot chick. I mean, I go for boys but in some weird way, I sometimes wanted to touch Marla, to kiss her. Above the waist girl love. There was one day when we lay on a lounge on the patio, and we were so close, and I wanted to kiss her, but I didn't. Then she reached for me, held me close and kissed me. Right on the lips and she opened my lips too. I pulled away at that point and said, "Come on. You know I'm not like that." And she just laughed in my face.

Marla was an only child, and you could tell that her parents spoiled her. But they also left her alone for long periods. "I used to have babysitters," Marla told me. "But then they decided I was old enough for them to just let me stay here."

I stayed over at her house a few times. We stayed up late and watched bad movies on TV and ordered pizza, took off all our clothes and squirted whipped cream on ourselves, made crank phone calls, and smoked the occasional joint.

I never told my parents that I was alone with Marla when I stayed over with her.

The house had a recreation room in the basement, with a wet bar. My dad mixed his cocktails on our dining room table, but Marla's dad could stand behind the bar and choose from the collection of alcohol on the shelf.

It was on a Saturday, shortly after school let out for the summer, when we gathered in the recreation room, just us four girls. The parents were off on a boat trip, according to Marla. She had invited me and Doreen over and Doreen, who was open-minded, had invited Janie to join us because Janie was small and shy and had told Doreen that she wanted to meet more girls and try to be popular.

I looked at Janie and thought she was an absolute cliché of the nerdy girl type. She didn't wear glasses, but she was nothing to look at.

"Let's have a drink," said Marla. She reached for the only bottle that was already open. It was vodka. She mixed herself a drink of vodka and ginger ale. "Moscow Mule, it's called." She offered to make them for all of us, but Janie declined. Little Ms. Innocent.

"We're not supposed to drink..." she protested, but Doreen groaned, and Marla rolled her eyes.

"No one's gonna know!" said Marla. "That's the point! Do you want to have some fun? Some real fun? Because I have an idea."

She explained that she was writing "assignments" on slips of paper. We had to draw the slips with our eyes closed, then read what the assignment was, and then go out and do it.

But the things we were supposed to do were forbidden things. Bad things. Crimes.

The rules of the game were simple. Each of us had to commit the crime written on the slip. At our next meeting each of us had to present proof that we committed the crime assigned to us. Anyone who didn't follow through on their crime would be expelled from the Canyon Crime Club, as we decided to call it.

Also, it had to be word of honor. Nobody snitching on anyone else.

***

We all got an assignment to tell a lie. That wasn't so bad. I lied all the time to my folks. I told them I was studying at friends' houses when I went out to movies and clubs. This time it was very easy to tell a version of that same lie, only I said I had gone on my own to a movie instead of saying that I had visited Marla.

Doreen told her boyfriend that she had been faithful, when actually she went on a date with some other guy.

Even Janie told a lie. She didn't tell her folks that she drank vodka for the first time with us that morning.

Marla told some complicated story about reading a letter addressed to her parents and replying to it when she was not supposed to. Bor-ing!

But you know, when she said the assignments were going to be fair, THAT was her lie!

DOREEN: I think I was flattered to be accepted by Marla. That was why I was willing, at first, to overlook the strange things about her, like how she was left alone so much by her family and how she said things to shock people.

She used to tell me stuff that sounded like lies all right. She said her father flirted with her. Used cuss words around her. I tried to seem like I wasn't shaken up. Her opinion of me went up a few points when I wore my mom's eye patch one day to look tough. After the pirate jokes died down, I explained that my mom has one eye as a result of a car accident, and it was her eye patch I was wearing. Marla liked that I did this. That's how you've got to be with Marla.

This assignment she had come up with was scary. But if I said I had doubts, I would lose her friendship and I didn't want to lose it. I would look like a coward and a nerdette. I think of myself as a sort of nowadays Beat Generation girl anyway, and I wanted to change my image a little bit.

We met at Marla's house a couple of days later. We had some sweet, awful wine and exchanged stories of our lies. Then

Marla gave us our next assignments. We all had to steal an item from our homes and exhibit it at our next meeting.

I stole a brooch from my mom's jewelry box. It was an emerald brooch that I had always wanted to have. I hated to not be able to keep it.

Lori stole fifty bucks from her dad's wallet. Janie was so silly. She stole a spoon from the kitchen. Marla scolded her for that, telling her she had to stop being a coward if she wanted to be one of The Bad Girls.

Marla showed us a check she had swiped from her mother's account. She was good at forging signatures.

I was worried about what we would have to do next. Somehow, I could not say what I was worried about. Marla had this way of looking at you if you got scared. She scared you even more. Did she scare me into what I did next? You bet your ass. Me, the pirate, the off-beat type. I'm a coward and I know it.

JANIE: I remember that after I told a lie and stole a spoon and they laughed at me, the next thing that Marla told me to do was to steal something from outside my home. Like from a store. I said I couldn't do it. Marla shouted at me: "You have no backbone!"

I cried and Marla kept taunting me, so I finally told her I would try.

Lori got "I will flirt with a man," which made her happy. She's a pretty girl so it would be easy for her. Doreen got the bad one. She had to hurt something or someone. Marla told her she could always step on a bug.

But Marla got a "control" slip. She had written on one of the slips "I will be good." And somehow, she got it.

JANIE: I went to this place in Santa Monica called Edgemar. Someone told me that it used to be dairy buildings, but it got converted into a sort of mall. There was a patio with a fountain and stores surrounding the patio. One store had odd toys and paintings. I still liked to look at toys. I longed to have a doll house. I'd never had one.

I thought of stealing a doll but that was so obvious and silly.

There was a humongous doll house with a high-ceilinged living room and avant-garde furniture designed by real designers. It also had artwork by real famous artists.

Nearby were small plastic bags of doll house furniture and accessories.

I grabbed one of the bags and stuffed it into my purse. I pretended to look at a few other items and snuck out of the store while the checkout lady was busy with a line of customers.

At home, I opened the bag. I had stolen a tiny coffee table made to look like a painted cable spool from the telephone company, a tiny chair with a slanted back, a sculpture of nothing (just shapes), a painting of colored squares (Doreen later said it looked like a Mondrian), and a very tiny black-and-white framed photo with a woman in the distance who looked like Marilyn Monroe but probably wasn't.

I felt a mixture of happiness that came from having furnishings for the doll house that I would someday own and guilt pangs over stealing them and worries about being caught. I knew Marla would laugh.

But when I emptied the bag in front of my three comrades in crime, they applauded me.

"Janie's got balls," said Marla.

"But it's just doll furniture."

"Are you kidding?" said Doreen. "That stuff is from the art doll house that they sell at LACMA. You stole a knockoff of a Mondrian. And the little photo looks like Cindy Sherman. You stole art, Janie! That's a major crime!"

I enjoyed being seen as gutsy by my peers. Doreen, on the other hand, had to exhibit a cockroach that she claimed to have squished (she told me later that her cat had actually killed it) while Lori passed around a selfie of herself with a good-looking young man who was grabbing her breast.

And Marla said, "I did nothing. I was good."

DOREEN: Then there was the meeting where Marla began to make the assignments tougher.

LORI: Are you sure? I thought we had a few easy ones and then she hit us with the tough one.

DOREEN: No, I know she upped the stakes after when you showed everyone that selfie. I remember she said, "Next time we are all going to get naked!"

LORI: Oh, right. Because Janie had a cow. She even crossed her arms over her chest!

DOREEN: Don't laugh. It wasn't funny.

LORI: I know, I know.

DOREEN: She handed us the slips and Janie suddenly said, "Let someone else hold them. You got the one about being good. It's not fair." Marla was like, how could you accuse me of not being fair? Janie said she wouldn't play.

LORI: And Marla reminded her that she had to keep the faith. And we reminded her.

DOREEN: I ended up shuffling the slips. I pulled the first one. It said, "I will have a lover."

LORI: And she wanted to know how to prove it this time. Marla said, "A used condom," and we all went "GROSS!"

DOREEN: I said, "I'll figure something out."

LORI: This time I got the one for theft. I had already stolen from my family. What did Marla expect this time?

DOREEN: I saw that Janie had gone catatonic. I asked her which one she had. She held it out for us to see. It was ridiculous. Marla had written "I will commit suicide."

I felt my stomach freezing up. I couldn't talk.

Lori said, "You aren't serious!"

Janie looked like she was going to burst into tears.

"Come off it," said Marla. "You don't seriously think you have to kill yourself?"

Janie shuddered. "How do I know?"

Lori suddenly got very protective of Janie and put an arm around her. Marla got that scary, commanding look on her face, just for a minute. Then she snapped her fingers.

"I've got it. You can cut your wrist. Then we'll bandage it up for you. You can even go to the E.R. if you need to. We'll say that you had an accident while you were cutting some veggies for a picnic."

"Marla, stop it," said Lori. "It's gone too far."

"Okay," said Marla. "Let's stop it. Sure."

She had that angry, bossy look that she always seemed to get when we refused to do what she wanted us to do.

"What are you all, a bunch of old ladies? We can't stop this," Marla continued, and her voice sounded darker. "I can make anonymous phone calls, you know. I could call the cops and give them a tip on who stole stuff from an expensive doll house."

I said, "I can't do this, either. It's sick. We have to stop."

Marla walked up to me and said, "Hey, Pirate."

Something inside me liked it when she called me a pirate. That eyepatch. Something inside me wanted to make her happy. Even if it was sick to do what she wanted me to do.

Marla put her arm around me. She petted my head like I was a cat. She smiled and used her most loveable-sounding voice:

"So, we're gonna do it one more time, right? This will be the last time. Janie, you don't have to kill yourself, just hurt yourself a little. Lori, my darling girl, go out and get it. Doreen, pirate, get over it and go have fun!

"Now, I just have to figure out how I will be good."

She was right about that!

***

LORI: I went to Santa Monica Place mall on a really hot afternoon. I kept going into the Starbucks and getting iced coffee to keep myself alert. I pretended to be looking at dresses and tops and earrings in various boutiques. I slipped several pairs of earrings into my purse. They were probably costume stuff.

I went into a big fragrance store. I would normally have hung out there just to sniff all the wonderful perfumes. But something got into me. It felt exciting to be bad. I didn't think about the future and getting caught. I was in the moment. The moment was a voice inside me, saying, "Just keep stealing! It feels like fun!"

I swiped a bottle of some knock-off of an expensive fragrance because the less expensive types were the only ones not kept in a glass case.

I waited until a clerk opened the glass case to give a woman a bottle of Opium. I went over to a shelf and knocked stuff off the shelf and yelled. This had the clerk running over to see what had happened. I grabbed two bottles of fragrance from the case and made for the exit. I ran so dammed hard that I was way out of breath. I thought I heard the alarm going off that signaled a shoplifter.

DOREEN: I got as relatively undressed as I could. I put on a tank top, striped horizontally, even though I always worry that I'll look fat with horizontal stripes. I combined this with a dark blue short skirt and blue sandals and turquoise earrings.

Then I thought that my legs weren't exposed enough. All the identifiable hookers I saw had bare, long legs. I changed to my shortest shorts. My hot pink shorts, to go with the red and white striped tank top.

I went to Santa Monica Pier. Normally, I hate the beach. I don't tan well. I walked along the pier, past the merry-go-round—nope, that's not a good place to pick up men. The other end, where they went fishing—no, there would be men there, but they'd smell fishy.

I walked down to the Ocean Front Walk where there was a well-known bar called Big Dean's. The men who hung out there were awful. Big, old, hairy, paunchy, with orange suntans.

I continued to walk south along the walk. I tried to do my best imitation of an Italian hooker in a foreign art house movie.

I had a continual feeling that this was a sick thing for me to do. I was almost ready to turn around and go home, admit to Marla and the others that I couldn't do it. I am not a slut. On the other hand, I'm not shy and I don't believe girls have to be virgins until they get married. But I do think there should be love with sex. This wasn't the way I had expected to have my first experience.

Why did I have to have this assignment? I bet Marla hoped she'd get it. Yeah, she would have loved to walk around and flash her body at men.

But I knew I had to be like an actress and play a role.

I smiled at men and they sometimes smiled at me, but mostly they went on their way. Just when I needed them to want to bother me, they didn't cooperate!

Finally, I just stood still and breathed heavily.

"Hey, you okay?"

It was a young man, a twenty-something skateboarder type of guy.

I smiled and tried to be provocative.

"I'm fine," I said. "Could you buy me a drink?"

"I don't drink."

"What? A cool-looking guy like you? Not even beer?"

"You want a beer? I'll buy you a beer."

"Never mind. You can buy me a latte."

A half hour later, we were in a motel room that he paid for. I began to wish I was drunk. I was cold sober and hated being in the room with him. I tried to pretend I was in a play or a movie.

Someone else gave him that hand job. It was all I could bear to do.

I had a tired hand. I washed up, wished him well, and left. There was still plenty of time to pick up another guy, someone I might feel something for. Then I realized I'd forgotten to get proof of what I'd done.

I was sitting on a bench, looking at the beach and the kids who were still innocent, when my phone rang. It was Lori. She'd been picked up for shoplifting.

JANIE: I was scared.

I didn't want to hurt myself.

Marla had the "I will be good" slip again.

How did she always end up with that one?

She had said it was supposed to be fair.

I went over to Marla's house.

She was alone again. Her parents never seemed to be around. Marla was in her room, lying on her stomach on the bed, reading a book with a dull gray cover.

"What book is that?

"It's essays, garbage for English class. This one essay is good, though."

I don't read many books. I can read better than they think I can but Marla, I knew, was a genius. "What does it say?"

"It's by this French guy. He talks about suicide and why people do it and then he talks about a man rolling a rock up a hill and it always rolls down again but he has to do it because it's a punishment for his sins and maybe he even enjoys doing it."

"It sounds silly."

"Of course, it's silly. He says it's absurd, is what it is. Suicide is absurd. That's why this is all supposed to be fake. I don't want you to kill yourself, Janie. We're just trying to see how far we can go."

"Like pushing a rock up a hill?"

Marla sat up on the bed. "Yes, exactly!"

"But I can't do it. It will hurt."

"You only have to cut a little bit. Like even a scratch."

"Are you crazy? What will my parents think? They already think I'm brain-damaged."

"That makes it better then, doesn't it?"

I felt my eyes tearing up. I cry a lot. I can't control it.

"Janie," said Marla. "You know we all swore on this. We can't break the faith."

"Then why don't we at least swap? Can't I be good, and you cut yourself?"

Marla looked disgusted.

We were both quiet for a while.

Finally, she said, "Okay. Be good. But you know, that means you cannot tell anyone. No parents, no police, anyone. If anything happens, if anyone discovers what we are doing, you have to be good and not say anything."

Marla took a small knife, the kind used for cutting fruit. I wanted to turn away, but she said, "You have to at least watch." She dug the point of the knife into her wrist. She pushed it farther in and blood began to show. I looked away again and she yelled, "You frigging coward, I told you to watch!"

"I don't want to see it. I hate blood."

"You don't even look at your periods?"

"I have to!"

Marla was smiling. She waved her bloody arm at me.

"Go to the medicine cabinet in the upstairs bathroom and get me a Band-Aid box and the Peroxide."

"But what about going to the E.R., like you said?"

"Just go!"

Marla was making me shake inside and outside.

I ran upstairs and looked through the medicine cabinet. Band-Aids. Band-Aids. Here they were. But what if it wasn't enough? I took a box of Band-Aids and some gauze and the peroxide, too.

When I got downstairs, I didn't see Marla.

She was not in the living room.

I walked into the dining room. No one there, either.

There was the study, but it was locked, and it was her dad's domain.

And, if you went down another flight of stairs, there was the rec room.

Something told me she would be down there.

I walked—no, ran down the stairs.

"Hold on Marla!" I shouted.

I ran into the rec room.

Marla lay on the floor. She was holding the small knife in her left hand. Her right hand was bleeding like crazy.

"Marla!"

"It won't stop," she whispered.

"Should I call emergency?"

"They'll know."

"But you said you would call if it was me."

"Don't call them. I don't want you to call them."

I took the knife from Marla's left hand and tried to bandage the other hand. I felt so nervous; my hands trembled, and I could hardly see what I was doing.

"Let it go, Janie. Leave me alone."

"No, Marla, please no."

"What do you care? I haven't been that nice to you or anyone. I hate all of you and everything. I hate life. Just let me die."

"I can't."

"Am I scaring you? You chickenshit, why are you always scared?"

"I don't know. Aren't you scared?"

"No. I want to die. Let me alone. Just go away."

I thought she was going to die. She was dying. I got my phone out and hit 911. I knew I was breaking our rules, but I said something about an emergency, gave the address, and fell down on the floor, too, gasping for breath.

I heard the front door of the house being opened. There were footsteps. From the floor, I looked up and saw Marla's parents.

DOREEN: I keep telling myself that this won't have to ruin all our lives. I've answered a thousand questions, been given tests, and I'm a genuine certified weirdo now. Maybe someday I will wear it like a badge. The counselor asked me if I'd like to go into her profession someday.

If I could see trouble coming in people and stop them before it gets bad, that would be something I could be proud of. I feel so ashamed, though, that I couldn't help Marla or Janie. Or myself.

LORI: We were all rounded up and questioned by the police and by youth officers. Our parents had to be brought in. My parents were disgusted. I was in a state of shock and sadness. I don't usually cry but I couldn't stop crying. I realized that I had become a juvenile offender. And that I had contributed to hurting others. And it wasn't sexy, and it wasn't funny. But it's Janie I really worry about.

They found her fingerprints on the knife. We told the police about the "assignments" on pieces of paper. But when the cops looked for the piece of paper with Janie's last "assignment," the one about suicide, instead they found a piece of paper that said, "I will kill someone." It was in Marla's writing. What did she do?

Please don't let them blame Janie.

JANIE: I don't know what to say. I don't know what I did. But I'm sorry.

I just know that when they helped me up from the floor I could only say over and over: "I was the one who was good."

THE WRITING ON THE WALL: A MODERN RETELLING

Shelley Burbank

Seated at a back table in the banquet room, Danielle Cunningham wondered if she could sneak away without anyone noticing. Dinner was almost over. The vaulted-ceilinged room of the newly opened Gaslamp Quarter hotel gleamed with gilded chairs, heavy purple draperies, and gold-and-glass chandeliers worthy of Louis XIV. At round tables squished into the room, two-hundred upper- and middle-level managers of The Felicity Organization and their companions finished off a heavy meal with a dessert course and coffee.

As desperate as she was to leave, she couldn't. The annual corporate party was compulsory, and if she left, some suck-up was sure to report it. The big boss, CEO Belto Shazner, styled himself as a benevolent dictator. His position was that employees *would* enjoy themselves at his banquet—whether they liked it or not. Danielle was definitely in the "not" category.

She'd come to the black-tie event alone. Her last relationship had ended badly, and she felt no great urge to begin dating again. Her thoughts hopscotched over that disaster to an earlier one, the relationship to which she compared all the rest. She pressed her lips together and pushed Maine—and the dangerous and unpredictable man she'd loved there—from her mind.

She didn't mind flying solo. It was safer this way. Truth be told, she preferred to spend her free time reading: novels and current event magazines, financial publications, esoteric white papers, and a few geopolitical and tech wonks in the blogosphere who were so far out on the fringes that very few people would recognize their names. Through these channels, she learned things, discovered layers beneath layers, and often correctly gauged the unpredictable.

She gazed at the bigwigs at the head table. She knew things about The Felicity Organization and Shazner, for instance, that most had no inkling about. Her boss stacked favors and deals like Jenga pieces. One wrong move and the tower would collapse. It was already swaying. Danielle planned to sit back and watch those pieces fall.

A burst of laughter erupted at the table behind her, and someone pushed out a chair, bumping the back of hers. She turned her head and gave the woman—Renee something or other from H.R.—a narrow-eyed stare. The woman shrugged and staggered off in the direction of the hotel lobby, probably in search of the powder room and a quick bump.

Danielle picked up her coffee cup. The man to her left said something to her. She nodded even though she'd only caught a fraction of his mumbled, bad-breathed comment. Over the rim of her cup, she spied a few members of the press, brought in, no doubt, to cover the event for *The San Diego Union Tribune* and a few local magazines that covered society news. The ostentatious fabric swags and gaudy floral arrangements, the gold flatware and ornate silver chargers were pure Belto, she thought. Showy. Wasteful. Tasteless.

Up on the dais, seated at the center of the head table, Shazner blathered on about corporate holdings, interest rates, ROIs, government regulations, overseas real estate markets, and company domination under his continued brilliant leadership. *So full of shit,* she thought.

Shazner was tall, an imposing six-foot-five. Seated on either side of Belto, beautiful women and men—The Felicity Organization's top executives and their domestic partners—gazed at Shazner as if he were a god. Or a king.

Danielle drained her coffee cup. She was twenty-nine years old, a few years out of a prestigious business school where she'd gotten a full-ride scholarship, thanks to her hard work and a determined advisor at her rural Maine high school. She'd been flown out to California a few weeks before graduation and given the hard sell and a generous offer. She'd accepted and had driven across country to the west coast as soon as she received her diploma.

Now employed as an internal accounting manager, she honed her skills while accumulating information, a kind of hobby. She was ambitious and had the brains to climb higher, but she kept her ambition to herself. Only a few trusted colleagues knew anything more about her than her last name.

At the bottom of the mid-level caste at Felicity, she'd created a camouflage of conservative corporate clothing, boring hair, and nerdy glasses. Her low-key suits were bespoke, London-tailored, impeccably fitted armor. Her mid-level cohorts only saw the bland shades of gray and navy blue, but beneath this nondescript exterior, she hid a sparkling intellect and a searing curiosity. She prided herself on knowing more than she let on.

Flying under the radar, she cultivated a network of associates inside and outside the company who dropped tidbits of information that she then put together, along with her internet browsing, into startling, often provocative insights. Nine times out of ten, her predictions panned out. She'd made a tidy sum playing the market. Nothing compared to the big, showy investors, of course, but enough to pay for the expensive but tasteful jewelry, shoes, and clothing.

Anyone could do the same, she thought. *Shazner, for example, if he'd stop thinking about himself and his so-called achievements for a minute and turn his attention to what was happening outside his corner office.*

Danielle had heard many quiet but disturbing rumblings lately, but Shazner appeared to have no idea just how shaky his position might be if one or two things fell into—or out of—place.

Finally, her boss came to the end of his speech. "And so, in celebration of a successful year, my friends, a toast. Bring out the Dom Perignon!"

Of course, he mentioned the brand, Danielle thought. *Total Shazner.*

People murmured and clapped as tuxedoed wait staff, bearing silver trays of champagne glasses, floated among the tables. Danielle grasped the stem of a delicate champagne flute. She clinked her glass to one side and then the other, and took a long sip. *Mmmm. Have to hand it to Belto, the bubbly added a nice touch.*

She took another appreciative sip but lowered her glass as gasps and murmurs erupted from the head table. Up on the dais, Shazner frowned, his face darkening. He looked over the heads of the crowd and pointed to the back of the room, spilling some of his wine. "What. Is. That?"

Heads whipped around. Danielle twisted in her chair. Above the tables, a cryptic message had been projected onto a white screen pulled down to float against the dark, fabric-covered wall. A photo of Shazner, graffitied with a tilted cartoon crown on his head and a sash pulled tight across his large gut reading "King Shaz," loomed above three glowing lines of script. The message read:

Beware the Dove that Nulls the Swan.

A Gold Goose nips the talons of the Hen

While the Partridge follows the Dove and Two Swans float away.

"What the hell's that bird nonsense?" Shazner's lapel mic picked up the annoyance in his voice. "Who's in charge of audio-visual? Darren? Get on it, will you?"

Darren Chang, vice president of communications, sprinted down and away from the dais.

Danielle took out her phone and snapped a photo of the image and message. Just in time, too, because a second later they went up in cartoon flames on the screen. Next, a series of photos flashed, one after the other:

Shazner with a hard-faced man Danielle recognized from her dark-web browsing as a minor Russian oligarch. Shazner in what looked like a Shanghai boardroom with several Chinese officials. Shazner smirking at the podium at some political fundraiser, jabbing a finger into the air, while behind him a wild-eyed crowd waved American flags.

The image faded and another took its place. A shadowy cartoon face whose grin widened until it took up the entire face, hovered like that of the Cheshire Cat, and faded to black.

Shazner sat down, shaking his head. CFO Clementine Dodson and Chief Legal Counsel Saquon Liberty pushed back their chairs and rushed to his side. Clementine leaned over the table, displaying more of her ample décolletage than she probably intended. Shazner, forgetting the hot mic, said to her, "What is this, a joke? Or is it some sort of threat? Clem? Am I in danger here?"

Around the room, people bunched together, and voices rose. Danielle looked up at the ceiling. The message seemed to have been projected from a complicated lighting device mounted above the dais. A few small indicators blinked green, red, green and went dark.

Chang appeared back at the dais with a hotel manager in tow. The manager lifted his hands, shrugged, looked up at the projector equipment. He shook his head and shrugged again.

Shazner's wife, former one-name supermodel Ashia, nudged Clementine aside.

Ashia put a hand on Shazner's shoulder. She whispered something in his ear, and he nodded before speaking again. "Okay, settle down everyone. Settle down." Shazner got to his feet. Ashia stood behind him, an impassive expression on her perfect features. "This message is probably a practical joke. A very bad practical joke. Nothing to worry about, folks. I want to find whoever set this up, doctored those photos. You know how they can manipulate photos now. And the message. Sounds like a lunatic to me. Some crazy nut-job trying to get under my skin."

Danielle watched Shazner's piggy eyes, squinting then widening with a kind of panic. "Here's what I'm gonna do. I'll give a substantial bonus—and a promotion—to anyone who can tell me who set this up and what it means. If it means anything."

Danielle sat back in her chair. Below the excited chatter in the banquet hall, a popular Christmas song had begun to run through her head.

A slight smile flitted across her lips, and she made a quick calculation.

She knew, or at least thought she did, the secret code the message contained. The question was, did she want to bring attention to herself?

Considering the situation, she waited a few minutes. Flying into Belto's radar might be more trouble than it was worth, especially because of the precarious position he and the company were in. She might be setting herself up for dismissal, harassment, or worse.

Still, it could be worth the risk. She'd had her eye on a new car, for one. The promotion, however, tempted her even more than the money, especially if what she thought was going to happen in the next weeks and months—namely a takeover and company restructure—panned out.

All the online gossip about Persius Tech she'd been seeing lately appeared to have merit. The dark web was full of speculation about Belto Shazner's dealings with foreign companies in states with questionable motives and he was suspected of meddling in American politics. Those photos projected on the wall had been a message. An "I know who you are and what you are and I'm coming for you" message. They were also leverage in case Shazner called on his political allies to help him out. No politician would dare to go to bat for him if those photos hit the mainstream media. And then there were the whispers about a shadowy shell company called Medena5 that'd been quietly positioning itself in the market. She'd been reading about all this for months, had been watching the market news, following the trends, biding her time. Now she was poised to reap the benefits of her nerdy, solitary pursuits.

Her eyes darted to the back wall, dark now, but she could still see it there. The Cheshire Cat smile. A different message. One possibly directed at her. *Possible, yes,* she thought. *But likely?* She didn't know. She'd figure that out later.

She turned her gaze back to Shazner. First things first.

Danielle stood and wound her way around the tables toward the dais. The room quieted. Someone laughed and was quickly shushed. Another person sneezed. Everyone was looking at her. Their gazes made her feel queasy, but she kept walking.

She came to stand below the head table. Shazner squinted down at her. "Who are you? Do you know something about this?"

"I'm Danielle Cunningham. From accounting. And, yes, I think so."

"Well, come on up." He gestured for her to step onto the stage. "Move over, Saquon."

Danielle walked up the stairs at the side of the dais and took the seat beside Shazner. Ashia watched her from beneath hooded eyes. Shazner made a rolling gesture with his hand. "Spit it out."

"Fine." She kept her eyes on his. Like most weak men, he despised the trait in others. If she showed fear, he'd dismiss her, and she could kiss the bonus and promotion goodbye. She took a breath and said, "I think it's a phone number."

"A phone number." He narrowed his eyes. "I don't get it."

Danielle pulled out her phone, showed him the photo she'd snapped. "I think it's a riddle based on the song, 'The Twelve Days of Christmas.' Notice the words that are capitalized? Each, with one exception, corresponds to a number in the song. 'Dove' stands for the number two. 'Null,' now that's the exception, but it means zero. Then there's 'Swan' for seven, and so on."

Shazner's expression was one of mingled admiration and skepticism. "Two-oh-seven. An area code?"

"Maine, I believe."

Shazner crossed his arms over his chest. "That's some crazy shit." He frowned. Drummed his fingers on the table. "I don't see it."

"Do you have a pen?"

Shazner looked around, made a gimme gesture to no one in particular. Saquon handed him a pen. Shazner gave the Montblanc to Danielle, who wrote the ten-digit number on the white tablecloth.

Shazner looked from the phone screen to the number to the screen again. He scowled up at her. "What the hell am I supposed to do with it?"

From behind him, Ashia held out a phone. She and Danielle exchanged glances. The corners of Danielle's mouth ticked up, but Ashia pursed her lips and looked away.

"Oh. Right." Shazner took the phone and then squinted, suspicious, at Danielle. "Pretty clever of you to figure this out."

"I am clever. That's why you hired me. You're good at finding the best."

He ignored the blatant suck-up and gave her a reptilian stare. "Maybe too clever."

A sick wave of panic rolled in the pit of her stomach. She talked fast. "Mr. Shazner, let me assure you, I didn't know anything about this before the words appeared on the wall a few minutes ago. I just have the kind of mind that can figure out puzzles and codes. Stuff gets in there, and well, gets trapped and filed and organized and connected. I'm wired for this stuff. Believe me, it's a curse as well as a gift."

"So, you really think this is just a phone number? And I'm supposed to call it?"

Her eyes slid away. "Well, depends on what you mean by *just* a phone number. It's a pretty elaborate prank. I think if you call the number, you'll hear a message. Or maybe you'll set in motion a series of events." She hesitated. "Or worse."

"You mean like a bomb or something?" He pushed the phone away from him. He clenched his fingers into a fist as if he were afraid they'd dial the number of their own volition.

"Could be. But if I had to wager on that, I'd say no. I think if you dial that number, you'll get a message from whoever set up this prank. But maybe to be on the safe side, don't do it right away. Not until security can check things out." She took a breath. "Anyway, if there is a voicemail for you on the other end, I think I know what you're going to be told."

"Which is?"

"Don't blame the messenger, but I think you're going to learn about a hostile takeover of Felicity by Persius Tech and Medena5. It's an investment firm."

Shazner froze. "I know what it is." He didn't look surprised or demand an explanation. Instead, he signaled to Saquon. "Contact Lawrence and Barbara. Tell them we need to check out Persius and Medena5, like, yesterday. We have to get out in front of this thing before Monday. I want the board and senior management at the office tonight. And we'll need support staff, as well." He pointed at Danielle. "And I want her personnel records on my desk in half an hour."

Saquon stood there, waiting for more instructions, but none were forthcoming. Shazner pounded the table in front of him. "Now!"

"Yes, sir." Saquon put his own phone to his ear and stepped behind the table to make the calls.

Danielle began to stand, but Shazner reached out and encircled her wrist with strong fingers. She tried to pull away, but he tightened his grip. He searched her face. "I'm going to run a background check on you, Ms. Cunningham. If you have something else you want to tell me, anything that connects you to this in any way, big or small, you'd better do it now."

Another rush of fear washed over her, but she held herself still and stared back at him. Look the predator in the face. Don't show fear. "I promise you. I had nothing to do with this."

"If that's true, I appreciate your coming forward. I'll see to it that you get your promotion and your bonus."

"Fabulous."

He glanced back at Ashia who then leaned down to whisper in his ear again. He nodded and stood. He lifted his hands to quiet the room. "Thank you everyone. I'm afraid the party's over. For your safety, I suggest you leave the premises. Do not talk to the press. Do not comment. Do not post about this on social media. If you've already posted on socials, delete. Immediately. You'll be updated on Monday. That's it. Thank you. Goodnight."

Everyone moved toward the exit. Shazner released Danielle's hand and she joined the crowd. She gathered her wrap from a coat-check attendant and walked out into a chilly, San Diego night.

By Monday, national and international media outlets broke the story of a hostile takeover of The Felicity Organization and of Belto Shazner's ousting by the new board. The following week, shocking revelations about Shazner's misuse of funds, embezzlement, tax evasion, and government bribes hit the news. Arrests were imminent.

Danielle never found out if Shazner called the number on the wall. She suspected he had. Ashia left the country before the arrests. Some suspected she'd been involved in the takeover, others that Shazner directed her to flee with her jewels and art. Still more whispered of secret, offshore bank accounts and foreign real-estate holdings.

None of Danielle's whisperers and informants knew what had really happened. It was a mystery and a puzzle, and, as a solver of puzzles, her mind had snagged on something and couldn't let go. That Cheshire Cat grin. She ignored it, feeling the less she knew, the better, but eventually temptation outweighed her survival instincts.

On a whim one lonely night a few months after the banquet, Danielle went to a dive bar in Ocean Beach, threw a twenty in front of the bartender, and asked to use the phone. She dialed the number. A recorded electronic voice said the number had been disconnected.

She ordered a dirty martini, drank it, and tossed down another twenty. She made a second call, this time to a landline number she hadn't dialed in years.

When a deep, familiar voice answered on the other end, she said, "Hi. It's me."

"Who's me?" The voice was teasing. He knew.

"Alice in Wonderland." She smiled. It had always been so much fun with him.

"Ah, so you figured it out."

"You knew I would, didn't you?"

"Want to meet?"

She signaled to the bartender for another martini. "Convince me."

The voice on the other end deepened. "You already called."

Damn. He was always one step ahead.

The next day, Danielle got into her new Mercedes and drove across the country, headed for a place called Gull's Haven, for a weekend rendezvous with her past.

CHILI CHEESE DOG

Wrona Gall

Lenny climbed out of the '67 red Corvette, wincing behind his Ray Bans. He liked his tan from a salon, not the August sun. Swiping the sweat from his forehead, he opened the steel-barred door and walked into Flash Cash. Every pawn shop smelled the same. Stale sweat and musty dirt overlaid with desperation. Lenny ignored this stench and focused on the cash that would soon fill his wallet. He ambled around the aisles to suggest an air of indifference. This casual attitude often raised his cut. When he felt the owner calculating his status as buyer or seller, he flashed the old Lenny grin that communicated both integrity and vulnerability.

The well-fed owner scratched the mosquito bites nestled in the American flag tattooed on his right arm. "So, what can I do you?"

Lenny took a hesitant step toward the wire cage, then stopped. "I inherited a watch, but to be honest, it makes me sad when I remember my mom wearing it. I thought I'd sell it and donate the money to a humane society. She was nuts about dogs, so it seems only right. I don't really need the money." Lenny watched the clerk take in the Burberry plaid collar on his shirt.

The clerk grunted his way up to a standing position. Lenny watched him flick his eyes over the Gucci belt around his impeccably tailored jeans. He might not be able to see Lenny's shoes, but he had to know the rest said money.

"I'm the one and only Manny Neumann, sole owner of this establishment. What do you go by?"

Lenny realized a chuckle would soften this guy up, so he made like a Comedy Club regular. The humor even reached his eyes. "Lenny Frank."

"Well, young man, let me see it." Manny leaned closer until his stomach scrunched onto the aqua-sparkled Formica.

Shoving a hand in his jeans pocket, Lenny dug out a Lady Rolex. He knew Manny would cheat him big-time, but when you acquire something at zero expense, breaking and entering—even twenty-five cents on the dollar brought a comfortable profit.

Manny unrolled a velvet jewelry cloth while keeping a neutral expression on his face. The five-figure value of the piece in front of him made this a challenge. Jewelry loop lodged in the pouches around his eye, Manny examined the watch. Breath scented with a lunchtime Pastrami sputtered from his fleshy lips. "You sure you wanna sell this? A Rolex-date-adjust-steel-yellow-gold-white-dial-ladies?"

Casting his eyes down to look sad, Lenny shifted his weight, working his soles into the gritted linoleum. Being a half-size too small, his Gucci loafers pinched his toes, but they were another "free" acquisition. He swallowed, then said, "Too many sad memories." He clamped his mouth shut. *Less said, more believed.*

Nodding, Manny offered an empathetic been-there expression. He held the watch up to the window. Light sparkled off the diamonds. "You got the real thing. Smooth second-hand movement." He hefted the watch in his hand. "Weight's right-on. Great winder. Look at those engravings." He rotated the watch. "Work of art. Even the date's magnified."

"Which all means my mom had good taste." Lenny was also mesmerized by the light reflections pinging off the diamond chips.

"And your pop had a thick wallet. You look like a smart fellow, so I won't snow you. Piece is worth three, four thousand retail. But nobody comes in here to pay retail. They go to Tiffany's to get the blue box. So, I can offer you...nine hundred. Any more and I can't pay my rent."

Lenny braced his jaw to keep his teeth from grinding. Of course, the guy was gonna screw him. "Can you come up five hundred, for the sake of those dogs?"

"Twelve hundred and that's it. Of course, I'll give you cash." Manny tugged at the gold cross tangled in his graying chest hair.

Drop dead and give the maggots a feast rolled around Lenny's mouth. He swallowed. "Deal." Like he had a choice. Big Ernie's guys told him they weren't waiting another day. And the last time he saw the big creep with the scar on his cheek, the guy looked like he was praying the Rosary that Lenny couldn't come up with the vig. Lenny crossed his fingers that the twelve hundred would buy him a couple weeks to make a bigger score.

Manny turned away from the steel-barred window and groaned his way to the back counter. His bulk eliminated any possibility that Lenny could read the combination of the safe Manny fingered. Off-key humming covered any clicks Lenny might overhear.

A rubber band snapped. Another. Paper landed on wood. Wheezing, Manny pulled up his pants and plopped his hip on the ripped vinyl stool. Pudgy fingers counted several bills on the counter, then slid them into the money slot.

A smile quivering the sides of his mouth, Lenny snapped up the bills. He shoved his salvation into his jeans pocket. Big Eddie's goons would have to find another punching bag.

Ignoring the red and white *No Smoking* sign, Manny picked up a cigar, rolled it around his fingers and snatched his lighter. "Good doing business with you, Lenny. Any other relatives join your mom, come see me."

Lenny gave a small salute, jingled the wind chimes over the door, then drove home, disappointed he hadn't scored more. He pried his too-tight shoes off his feet, rubbed his toes and plopped onto his burgundy velvet recliner. Time to moonlight again. Booting up his computer, Lenny accessed the Deluxe Travel site he'd hacked into a month earlier.

He skimmed the options. A couple at a Cancun resort for seven days. Their Koreatown address wasn't promising. A doctor on a ten-day tour of the Amazon rain forest. Last doctor he hit had a patient emergency and came back five days early. Lenny'd barely escaped out the back door when the guy came screaming in the front. A women's book club on a week's trip to New York. They all probably kept their faux jewelry in pink leather boxes with dancing ballerinas on top. *No way.*

Bingo! A lawyer, Rick Menter, La Jolla address, had booked a two-week Royal Caribbean cruise to Alaska. He checked out the house. *Wonderful.* A vintage sixties ranch. Probably hadn't been renovated in decades, which meant ancient plumbing. He'd pack his picks, slap his *Smooth Flow Plumbing* sign on a van he'd boosted, and "inherit" some jewelry and probably a bundle of cash from the guy's safe.

But first he'd do his due diligence—those words made him feel so professional—and case the joint to check out the security and make sure no one was house sitting at night. He grabbed his helmet and a paper-stuffed Fed Ex box, then walked three blocks to the vape shop that rented him parking spaces for two-fifty a month. His Harley was gassed and ready to go so he arrived at Rick's fifty minutes later. He parked in the narrow driveway in front of the garage and walked across a manicured lawn.

Scanning the area, Lenny pulled the envelope from under his windbreaker and hurried to the front door. A video camera drooped from its bracket. He banged the front door and turned his face away even though he still wore his helmet. An ADT sign marred with rust hopefully meant the guy had canceled the account years before.

He shifted from one foot to the other, feigning impatience. Finally, he tore a pink sheet off a message pad, scribbled Failed Delivery followed by a fake number. He stuffed the note behind the door handle, then spun out of the driveway.

On his way home Lenny couldn't stop thinking that lawyers always had safes. They didn't trust nobody, no way. Inevitably safes were hidden behind a painting or under a rug in the master bedroom or home office. A big score from a safe could pay off his bills and leave enough cash to hang out at Del Mar Racetrack for a day.

The next three hours were taken up with his "visual transformation." He'd heard that in a movie once and liked it way better than "putting on a disguise." A blonde wavy wig hid his crewcut. Brown contacts transformed his hazel eyes. A spider tattoo wrapped its web under his right ear to create a focus. If anyone became suspicious of his arrival or departure, the arachnid would definitely dominate their description.

Mascara smudged his left cheek and dirtied his fingernails. Gray coveralls slouched over his worn black work boots. His picks went into his right pocket, his burner cell landed in his left. He pulled a Padres hat low over his forehead, snapped on plastic gloves and picked up a battered metal tool case. Off for an easy night's work.

Darkness shrouded the garage behind the vape shop. Lenny unlocked the two padlocks on his space, slapped his plumbing sign on the van's door and revved the engine. Two a.m. meant less traffic, so it only took him thirty minutes to reach Rick's place. Low black lights still lined both sides of the driveway. He parked, grabbed his tool box and hiked toward the front door. This should be an easy in and out. Neighbors shied away from a plumbing truck like it was contagious or something. Even better, places like La Jolla ignored anything that wasn't all about them, so nothing would infringe on their sunny paradise. Calling the cops—and getting involved in a tedious conversation—qualified.

Car lights flashed across the street then disappeared around the corner. Swinging his toolbox, Lenny approached the massive oak door, which was fortified with a vintage cast-iron lock. Just in case the camera worked, Lenny kept his face turned away while he picked the lock in a personal best of three minutes. Inside, he tensed for an alarm beeping but only heard the creaks he created crossing the oak flooring.

Carved wood panels covered every vertical surface. An antique oak armoire spread across the wall opposite a picture window shadowed by gold damask drapes. Green velvet couches anchored the glass coffee table with what looked like a huge rock in the middle. He poked it with a gloved hand and the thing toppled. Weird, it only weighed a few pounds. He toed an old-fashioned light timer. Lenny snorted, gleeful that rich bastards could be so damn cheap about security.

A bathroom squeezed between the formal living area and a dining room that was crowded with a dozen high-backed chairs around an oval mahogany table. Shelves filled with dishes bracketed a swinging door opening to a stainless kitchen like a Home Depot display. A window offered a view of a backyard studded with cement planters overflowing with some kind of red flowers.

Lenny continued down a hallway lined with big paintings of squiggles and smears. A small guest room on his right held a twin bed with a white bedspread. Guests must not be too important because the only other furniture was a small dresser holding a lamp with a black shade.

A closed door on his left loomed ahead. Lenny turned the knob and entered a master bedroom with a king-sized bed overwhelmed by an avalanche of black and white pillows. A TV was installed above an eight-drawer dresser. And the en suite hosted a walk-in shower bigger than his kitchen.

No office. The moon cast a subtle glow across the room. Lenny looked behind paintings and scuffed his toe on the hardwood floor that couldn't hide even the smallest safe. That left the bookcases. He sifted through books and moved a couple of bronze sculptures that looked like lumps of mud. Nothing. That left the closet.

Rick had taste. Cashmere sweaters, suits with labels from Gucci to Versace. But something seemed off. He paced the space and realized the left clothes rod appeared to be about a foot closer to the wall than the right. He tapped the paneling: Solid, solid, hollow.

He knew it. Rick's hiding place. Lenny ran his palms against the wall but couldn't find a switch or button. Then he thought higher tech. He dug through every pocket of every frickin' jacket and shirt and pants to find a remote. Nothing.

Frustrated, he kicked the shoe rack. Gucci loafers—not second-hand, he'd bet—and Michael Jordan sneakers jumbled together. A pair of black riding boots didn't even sway. Lenny grinned like a jackal spying a rabbit.

He shoved one hand into each boot, betting on the left. He lifted, twisted then pressed down. Nothing. Then he dragged off his Skechers and slid his feet inside the boots. A click, then the wall behind the clothing slid to the left. *Open Sesame.*

Narrow steel shelving lined the back wall. Lenny reached for his tool case and dumped the contents on the carpet. If he got caught on the way out, tools wouldn't disguise his break-in. He opened a box and admired a set of gold cuff links and several pinky rings imbedded with various colored stones. If they were real, the emeralds and rubies were as good as the gold. Papers stuffed an expanding file. He tossed everything in the tool case, secured the locks, then retreated from the closet.

Lenny bolted to the exit, then slowed to carefully unlock the front door. He walked out, then stuck his head back in like he was speaking to someone. Pulling the door shut, he forced himself to stroll to his van. He got in the driver's seat, attached his seat belt, and drove away, maintaining the speed limit until he parked at the vape shop.

It took him ten minutes to hurry back to his house. Grabbing a beer, he settled on his couch, opened his tool case, and rifled through the accordion file. A manila envelope slipped out. He ripped it apart. A pile of fifties fell on his lap. He counted $600, then tossed the bills on the table next to the beer bottles. A white leatherette notebook listed birthdays and anniversaries for either clients or friends. Maybe both. The notebook wobbled a beer bottle when it joined the money. Lenny untied the expanding file and whooped with delight when he scanned the first page. A spreadsheet of bank entry dates, phone numbers, addresses and initials confronted him. *Hot damn.* The holy grail of a blackmailer. Old Rick hadn't earned his house in a courtroom.

Checking the amounts, he saw DB was evidently kicking in the most—five hundred bucks a month to Rick's household budget. There were fifteen sets of initials down to one-fifty from a JH. It looked like all Lenny had to do was decipher the names and he'd have more than enough to fund his lifestyle. He scanned the rest of the pages but found nothing interesting. Annoyed, he got up for another beer. The briefcase landed on the floor. He kicked it out of the way, then grinned. An external drive nestled in the orange shag carpeting.

The hell with a beer. He grabbed his laptop and inserted the device. It clicked. Lenny tapped it open. The page filled with names, numbers, and addresses next to individual photos. Rick was one organized guy. First name, Deborah Barcley. A fiftyish-sixtyish woman who lived in La Jolla and was trying to turn back the clock with rainbow hair, a facelifted smile that barely stretched her lips, and enough makeup to make a Mary Kay rep swoon.

What had little Deborah done? He scrolled through the rest of the pages. Deborah had embezzled over two million dollars from the Save the Migrant Children Foundation she had founded. If anyone learned her secret, she'd not only be broke, but Facebook and Twitter would tell the world she was lower than pond scum. No wonder she was paying Rick five bills a month. Maybe he should research the other names on the list and see if Deborah was the best choice. Then he thought about Big Ernie's goons and plowed ahead.

No time like the present. He grabbed his burner and tapped in her number, 858—somewhere San Diego—and a bubbling voice answered. He introduced himself as a concerned friend, rushing his words before Deborah could speak.

"I'm taking over. You'll be making your payments to me

from now on."

"I have no idea what you're talking about. Don't ever call me again. I can track this number so get lost. Or better yet, drive off a cliff."

"I got your number from Rick."

He heard a gasp, then a splutter. "I'm not paying you and Rick both."

"Don't worry. Rick's out of the picture. I have all his records. It'll be the same payment, just to me."

"The usual post office box?"

"Not this time. Just this once I need the payment early. Tomorrow morning." An earsplitting screech made Lenny drop the phone. "What the hell, lady. It's just two weeks early. Where are you?"

"None of your damn business."

"Keep your panties on. I know you're from San Diego County. Go to Original Tommy's and buy a chili cheese dog and fries. Put the money under the food and refold the bag. Then go to Del Mar Dog Beach. Park near Peñasquitos Lagoon. Leave the bag to the right of the men's room. My guy will be watching, so don't try nothing cute. Got it?"

"Got it, as you say. Except where the hell am I going to find an Original Tommy's?" Deborah sounded like his ex-wife when she kicked him out of the house.

"Google it. Remember tomorrow morning. Ten sharp."

"Like I have a choice. I'll be there. Just know I hope you rot in hell."

"You never know."

Lenny disconnected, treated himself to a celebratory beer, then set an alarm on his phone for seven. It would give him plenty of time to put on his disguise, get to the beach and find a good surveillance spot before Deborah arrived.

He surprised himself by dozing right off and sleeping through to the next morning. Completing his disguise, he dressed in a navy T-shirt and tan cargo shorts, even though he was as bowlegged as a rodeo rider. *Important to blend in.*

Lenny hurried to the vape shop, rode his Harley to the beach, and luckily found a close parking spot in case he had to make a fast getaway. He sat on the bike, tattooing the handlebars with nervous fingers until he realized he was looking way too obvious. He strolled to the far side of the restrooms and texted Big Ernie's guys to meet him at the beach. This way he could pay them off and get to the first race at the Del Mar Racetrack.

His vape pipe kept him calm until a Red Audi TT coasted to a stop several cars behind his bike. The woman in the picture stepped out of the car, dressed head to toe in black with matching hat and sunglasses. She used both hands to clutch a white bag with red lettering. Her remote beeped. It was Deborah all right.

She marched across the parking lot, head swiveling until she arrived at the restrooms. She stooped and tucked the bag to the right of the men's room, then stilettoed back to her car.

As soon as she squealed out of the space, Lenny appeared from the far side of the men's room. He strolled to the door, adjusted his helmet, and leaned down. Tommy's chili scented the air. A scream pierced the park. Lenny leapt up and looked around. An animal torpedoed toward him. "What the hell?"

A German Shepherd trailing a pink leash slammed into him. He fell back. Enormous jaws enveloped the bag. Lenny kicked his boot at the dog. He missed. The dog leapt away, saliva drenching the red lettering.

A scream of rage assaulted Lenny. "Leave Sweetie alone, you brute." An arthritic woman trotted up to Lenny and bashed her walking stick against his helmet.

"You bitch. That's my bag." Lenny raised his fist to fling the woman aside.

She shoved her cane in his face. He grabbed the stick and threw it behind him. Whirling around, he pounded after the dog. Massive arms dragged him back. Big Ernie's scar-faced guy glowered at him.

"You mugging a little old lady?"

Lenny cringed, pointing at the dog, whose tail was disappearing along the beach path.

"The money."

"Is overdue." Big Ernie's guy rubbed his scar.

"Holy hell."

LIFE ON THE RANCH, SOUTHERN CALIFORNIA STYLE

C.C. Guthrie

It was distrust at first sight between OB MacMartin and Captain Jason Westover. The blazing sun and heat only added to the tension. Westover sported half-moon underarm sweat stains on his summer shirt. The standard-issue sheriff's uniform was more suited to his previous post in the urban part of the county.

In our precinct to the east, four-wheel drives with heavy-duty winches on the front and snakebite kits in the back were necessities. Deputies out here sneered at colleagues who patrolled the beaches and parks on bicycles and called it "Southern California Riviera" duty.

Once Westover found out that the Old Bastard and I had been in the presence of at least fifty people for the two hours preceding Roy Natterly's death, he interviewed us together, probably thinking that OB would behave himself with me beside him. Westover had a lot to learn.

"Ms. Taylor, why did the employee who found Natterly notify you first, instead of calling nine-one-one?"

With unexpected speed, OB sprang to my defense. "Lay off her. Kit's my Operations Manager. She's the boss. Of course, the crew would call her. Besides, once she confirmed Natterly was dead, she called nine-one-one."

Apparently, all it took for OB to back me up was murder. My grandfather wasn't known for his effusive praise.

Westover seemed unimpressed by OB's support, so I didn't bother to mention the size of the annual budget I managed or bring up our year-over-year profits.

With nothing left to badger me about, Westover switched his attention to OB.

"Mr. MacMartin, you had a history with the deceased. I'm told that you once took an ax to the victim's house, used it to hammer on his front door, and threaten him."

OB shook his plastic cup as if that would conjure up another serving of his favorite craft beer and grinned at the memory. "Damn straight. It was ten—?" He looked at me.

"Twelve."

After OB gave me a slow wink, he continued. "Twelve years ago, that idiot Natterly, or one of his no-good spawn, cut my fence. Eight steers got out on the road. Lucky none were hit. Told him if he ever damaged my property again, I'd damage him." OB lifted his chin at Westover. "Haven't had to go back since."

"So, what caused you to kill Roy Natterly today?"

With his characteristic snarl, OB gave as good as he got. "If you believed I killed that no-good waste of oxygen, then you'd have already hauled me out of here in cuffs. You should interview a few more people before you finalize your suspect list."

The sweat stains on Westover's shirt crept lower. We sweltered in the still air at a dinky table under a nine-by-nine popup canopy that I'd graciously asked my crew to set up so Westover could conduct interviews. Twenty feet away, guests of the MacMartin Enterprises Appreciation Calf Fry sat in the big marquee tent that we used for our event. The two Friggin Big Fans we'd brought in might not have cooled down the space, but at least they generated a breeze.

Westover turned his attention back to me with a glare that might have made a bikini-clad tourist nervous. After living and working with OB, I was immune to intimidation.

"You should listen to OB. Natterly wasn't liked or respected by anyone."

"If you had issues with the victim, why did you invite him to your barbecue?"

Westover's question sent Fourth-of-July-sized sparks shooting out of the thought bubble over OB's head. "It's a calf fry, Captain, not a barbecue. I thought you city folk were foodies. Even you should know cooking over a fire is different from frying." OB clutched his empty cup a little tighter. "Kinda like how steers and bulls are similar but different." He sat back, eyes half-closed, scorn on full display. Westover matched OB's expression.

That left me to make the explanation, of course. "Our core business is cattle, specifically, steers. During the year, we acquire bulls, convert them, and accumulate a steady supply of raw material that we fry up at our annual event."

Unsure if Westover got it, I cut to the chase. "Calf fries are also known as lamb fries, prairie oysters, Rocky Mountain oysters, tendergroins, cowboy caviar, swinging beef, or dusted nuts. They're bull testicles."

Westover passed a hand across the greasy sheen on his forehead and dislodged two drops of sweat that rolled down each side of his tanned face, a shade lighter than it might have been before I explained about calf fries. To give him credit, he recovered quickly.

"Interesting menu. People out here eat that, do they?" he asked.

OB's chin shot up. "Some do, some don't. I also serve tri-tip and a few vegetarian and vegan dishes, along with sides. Gotta roll with the times."

Family loyalty required that I chime in with a brag. "Our calf fry is known all over Southern California. It's an annual event to thank our friends, neighbors, and business associates for their support."

OB nodded. "Got some big-name Hollywood types that come, some Orange County politicians, college professors. Hell, somebody even brought along that whiz kid property developer making news. Although, if you asked me, he's got a lot to learn about life out here." OB pointed at me. "Kit, what was his name again?"

"Matthew Tyson."

"He's a little odd. Don't think I'll invite him next year."

Westover's left eyelid flickered. "Odd? What do you mean?"

"Showed up looking like a goofball," OB said. "If he wants to do business with folks in this area, he needs to fit in. His outfit was like wearing a sign that said, 'I'm not from around here.'"

"What did he wear?"

I gave OB a side-eye and tried to downplay the criticism. "Golf clothes. They were a bit on the colorful side." OB was right. It wasn't a winning strategy for someone looking for clients in our part of the county.

Tired of the fashion critique, Westover returned to the reason for our chat. "Back to my question. If you and your neighbors didn't like or respect Natterly, then why did you invite him today?"

OB waved his arm around, suggesting that he spoke for everyone within hearing distance. "Civility." He grinned. "Besides, Natterly, being the type of person he is, or was, I wanted him pissing out of my tent, not into it."

Westover put down his pen. "What was he like?"

"Lazy, no-good, con man, always puffing himself up to look smarter and more important than he was," OB said. "Out for a quick buck. No one took him seriously."

"Tell me about the cons."

OB glanced up as if the list was printed overhead and then looked back at me. "What was that deal about him being a land-finder?"

There were so many stories about Natterly, it took me a few seconds to dredge that one up from my memory. "A while back he called himself a land scout and offered his services to a couple of real estate agencies in town."

"Doing what?"

"Wanted to sell tip sheets listing elderly landowners whose heirs weren't in the area and would likely sell up when their relative kicked off."

Westover looked confused. "Don't agents around here already know that?"

OB laughed and pointed his index finger at the captain. "Bingo. That sums up how Natterly thought. Get paid for nothing."

"OB, ever notice Natterly always hinted that he knew things no one else did? What if he demanded money to keep quiet?"

Westover sat up straight and all but sniffed the air like a bloodhound that caught an intriguing scent. "Blackmail?"

I looked at OB and we shrugged.

Westover pulled out his phone, tapped, and scrolled. He started to give it to OB and changed his mind. "Ms. Taylor, does this mean anything to you?"

I enlarged an image of names, each one followed by a string of letters, numbers, and slash-marks. I handed the phone to OB. He looked, nodded, and handed it back to Westover.

"Do you know what that means?" OB asked him.

Westover surprised me by answering honestly. "No. Do you?"

"Those are legal land descriptions. Probably property owned by those people. Their deeds would confirm that."

"We found that list on Natterly," Westover said. "Could it be one of his tip sheets?"

OB looked dubious. "Why carry it around if no one wanted to buy it?"

Westover reached into his breast pocket, retrieved a small notebook, and flipped to a page. "Your address is 10986 Crest Ridge Road. Why isn't that the legal description? Why complicate things with all those letters, numbers, and slashes?"

I sent OB a frantic brain-to-brain message to be kind with the lecture that I knew was coming.

"We only got addresses out here like city folk back in, jeez, I don't remember," he said. "But that's just so your deputies, the fire department, and EMS can find us." He flicked his wrist at Westover's phone. "A couple of hundred years ago, surveyors created a system to map undeveloped land and describe property boundaries where there weren't permanent landmarks like roads or city blocks. That's what those letters, numbers, and slashes mean." He sat back in his chair with a thump and exhaled, the signal that he'd run out of patience. "If you want the history of the Section, Township, and Range system, Google it."

To lower the temperature, I stepped up again. "What does any of this have to do with Natterly's murder?"

"Good question," Westover said. He gestured at his phone. "Know anything about the people on the list?"

I pointed to three names. "They're dead."

That perked Westover up. "Suspicious deaths, were they?"

OB looked bored and shook his head. "Nope. Pneumonia, T-boned by an eighteen-wheeler, and complications after hip surgery."

Westover wasn't pleased that OB poked a hole in that line of investigation and let us leave, although he insisted one of his deputies escort us back to the marquee as if we couldn't be trusted to walk the twenty feet. While we'd been gone, someone in the tent shifted all but two of the tables into half the available space.

OB looked at the lopsided arrangement and back at our minder. "What the hell did you do that for? Folks are crammed in so tight, they're likely to suffocate."

"Sorry, Mr. MacMartin. We need to keep the people who've been interviewed from talking to the ones who haven't." Sergeant Kenny Fujihara looked apologetic but wasn't cowed by OB's snarl. It was a different story back when OB caught Kenny sneaking me home at two in the morning after our junior prom. OB yelled, Kenny quivered, and I tried not to laugh.

As directed, OB and I sat alone on one side of the tent, and I counted heads on the other. Including our employees, there were only sixty people. I wondered if the other guests left before Natterly was killed, or before Westover and his team showed up.

OB looked longingly at the beer kegs that were off-limits and sighed. "What happened to Jenny? She should have been here by now."

I'd been asking myself the same question. Jenny Carter was an old friend and the niece of our neighbor, Hugh Miller. She was the executor of her uncle's estate and was flying in to see the attorney handling the probate. Even factoring in a rental car pickup and traffic, she should have arrived by now. A check of my phone confirmed that she hadn't called or sent a text.

OB jabbed me in the ribs. "You got a copy of that guest list in your pocket?"

"Nope."

He frowned at my dereliction of duty. "Look over there and tell me who's missing."

Our crew sat at one table, and neighbors and town folk at another. The feed company rep, the owner of the largest tractor dealership in the county, and our veterinarian-supply account manager sat together. At another table were a couple of local politicians and area bigwigs. My eyes passed over them, and then I went back for another look. "Earlier there were four bankers there; now there's only one, and she looks pissed."

OB laughed. "Well, I 'spect she's a bit uncomfortable, what with sitting beside his honor's wife. The judge can't be very happy about that, either."

It took a second for OB's hint to register. "Do you mean what I think you mean?"

He gave me a sly grin. "Straight from Natterly's mouth."

"Huh. Natterly was sitting at that table earlier. When I passed by, he said something about deeds."

"What about them?" OB asked.

"Not sure. I only caught a few words. Hell, knowing Natterly, he might have been recruiting partners for one of his cons."

OB brushed off the idea with a flick of his wrist. "Sounds

like him, but he could only scam people in cities, where no one knows each other. Out here, everyone pays attention to who owns what and what it's worth."

OB made a good point. Nothing got past our neighbors.

"Why didn't you tell Westover what you heard Natterly say?"

"Must have been the heat. I forgot until just now. If it had been anyone other than Natterly talking, I'd have paid more attention."

OB winked. "Hey, if one of those bankers is into land fraud, maybe they knocked him off."

"Good theory." I stood up and stretched. "Want a bottle of water?"

Three steps from the table, I remembered there was only melting ice in the galvanized tubs at the back of the tent. Earlier, I'd sent an employee to the warehouse for more water, but when he made a detour behind the building for personal business, he found Natterly's body.

"I'll see if Westover will let me go to the warehouse."

"Send Dougie," OB said.

"I'll go too, I'm tired of sitting."

I explained to Kenny about the water and suggested that he come along to reassure Westover that we weren't messing with the crime scene.

We were halfway to the shade canopy when a sheriff's vehicle pulled up, and out popped Jenny. I was amused to see that the driver was Michael Mata, her crush when we were sixteen. To her chagrin, he was focused on summer league baseball and barely noticed her.

Before I could hug Jenny, Westover stepped between us and then directed his ire at Michael. "Why is she here? I said no one else gets in."

The vein on Michael's forehead signaled a warning that Westover ignored. "She says she's Mr. MacMartin's guest."

Westover ordered me back to the marquee tent, but I wasn't

having it. "Captain, it's hot and we've run out of water. Can Dougie Carstairs and I go down to the warehouse for a few more cases? There's plenty of room for either Sergeant Fujihara or Deputy Mata to go along."

Unhappy that I'd forced him to make a decision, Westover looked at Kenny, who signaled approval with a slight lift of his chin. Westover then reasserted his authority and waved over a third officer. "Deputy Naki, I need you to go with Ms. Taylor and her foreman."

I gestured at the marquee. "Can I get Dougie?"

Ever prissy, Westover insisted on issuing more orders. "Deputy Naki will escort you to your vehicle, and Deputy Mata will get Mr. Carstairs."

As soon as Dougie joined us, I gave Jenny a warning look and she retreated under the canopy. Westover remained where he was, arms crossed, the dictionary definition of irritation. I hit the power pedal on the electric cart, and we were off, leaving Westover in a cloud of dust.

Once out of his view, Deputy Naki turned to Dougie. "What you got yourself messed up in, cuz?"

I laughed and gave her a poke in the arm. "Jeez, Chrissy. Your new boss is a jerk. Who peed in his cornflakes?"

She grimaced. "I doubt he'll last more than two years out here, but until then, I think I'll transfer to the Riviera and work on my tan."

I concentrated on driving, worried that I'd turn us over on the rutted old fire break road, while Dougie and Chrissy talked about the effect the heat and drought had on livestock and wildlife. As we neared our storage buildings, two foxes that OB, Dougie, and I'd been observing for signs of stress gave us wary looks before darting off.

"They seem to be doing okay," Dougie said. "Let's move the critter cams to the north pasture. There's a doe and her fawn that need watching."

We made it to the warehouse without a mishap and Dougie

leaped out to key in the code for the roll-up door. Still parked off to the side of the building were two sheriff's vehicles. Four deputies methodically searched the pasture behind the warehouse. Chrissy and Dougie joined me to watch.

"Searching for the weapon?" Dougie asked.

Chrissy's neutral expression didn't give anything away.

Then I stuck my foot in it. "Probably trying to figure out where Natterly was killed."

She jerked around and gave me a sharp look.

I put up my hands. "Hey, I saw Natterly's head. There wasn't much blood around."

She raised an eyebrow.

"Don't look at me like that. It's because of you that I know head wounds bleed a lot. Remember the dodgeball game when you fell into the bleachers? Your head bled so much it looked like we'd butchered a cow in the gym."

She let a beat pass, then grabbed Dougie and me by our arms and led us back to the warehouse. "Get your water. I don't need the new boss on my back before my transfer to the Riviera goes through."

Westover must have sped through his interviews while we were gone because we returned to a nearly empty marquee. Dougie and I iced down the water and took bottles to OB and Jenny.

"Did you know that Jenny got a text from Natterly?" OB asked.

"Why would he do that?"

"I have no idea," she said. "When my flight landed, I had a message but didn't know who it was from or what it meant." She pulled out her phone, tapped, and held it up so I could see the screen.

You been cheated. See me at MacMartins. RN

I looked over at OB. "Natterly always did think he was the center of the universe. Typical of him to assume Jenny'd know who RN referred to."

"Speaking of unknown people," she said. "A guy named

Matthew Tyson called me last week to ask if I'd sell Uncle Hugh's land."

"Did you agree?" OB asked, not hiding his anger.

"Of course not," she said with a bite in her voice. "According to my attorney there's a problem with the deed and I can't sell yet."

OB huffed. "There's no damn problem with the deed. Hugh inherited that land from his father, just like I did from mine. When you're ready I'll buy everything and that'll save you a real estate commission. But I don't see what any of this has to do with Natterly."

Jenny looked frustrated. "I don't either. Who was this Natterly person?"

I touched her hand. "He was the mean guy that we used to mess with every summer. The one that lived down the road from Hugh and Millie."

Jenny and I met when we were eight, the first of many summers that she and her brothers spent with their aunt and uncle who lived in the next section over. The boys, two and three years older, didn't want us tagging along on their adventures, but when it came to getting back at Natterly, the four of us joined forces. He was a jerk, even back then. If he saw us riding our bikes, he'd swerve his beater truck as if to hit us, and he used to shoot his shotgun into the woods when Jenny's brothers were playing there.

"That was crazy man's name? Natterly?"

OB's head jerked up. "You swore you kids weren't the ones going onto his property."

I tried to look contrite but didn't feel it. "We lied." What we'd done was mild, even by the standards back then. We regularly egged his house, the ammunition filched from Natterly's hens. Laundry left on the line overnight was moved to high limbs on nearby trees. There was so much crap on Natterly's property, it was easy to hide his kids' toys.

Although relieved to find out who RN was, Jenny still had

questions. "Why did Natterly send me a text about being cheated, and how did he get my cell number?"

I pulled out my phone. "Look, all these websites claim to reveal private details about people for a fee. And no, I don't know where they get the information. But something Natterly saw made him suspicious. And remember, your attorney found something iffy about Hugh's deed, too."

OB harrumphed. "Hate to give that bastard any credit."

"Assuming someone pulled a fast one with Uncle Hugh's land, who did it?"

"That's the million-dollar question," OB said. "But I'd bet that same million that Natterly made someone nervous when he started talking about deeds today."

Dougie and Jenny looked confused, so I told them what I'd heard.

"Isn't it likely someone at that table killed Natterly?" Jenny asked me.

"Not necessarily. Anyone walking by could have overheard what he said, and who knows who was at the table, the way people roamed around and table-hopped."

Even OB agreed with me on that point.

"But Natterly was such a blowhard," Dougie said. "No one around here would have taken him seriously."

Westover walked into the tent, and we all went on guard.

"Mr. MacMartin, tell me about the small building next to your warehouse."

Dougie, OB, and I exchanged looks.

"It's storage for spare parts, things we might need," OB said.

Dougie laughed. "It's all crap."

The argument was an old one, repeated every few years. Dougie and I wanted to clear out the building and OB was adamant we wouldn't. Most of the stuff had belonged to his grandfather and father.

"Why do you want to know about the building?" Dougie asked.

"It's now central to our investigation."

I flashed back to the dead man's battered head. "Oh, jeez. Was Natterly killed in the parts shack?"

Westover gave me the same look that Chrissy had when I suggested Natterly wasn't killed in the pasture behind the warehouse.

"Tell me more, Ms. Taylor."

For the second time, I insisted that I was only guessing. "Given the severity of his head wound, there wasn't much blood nearby."

Westover's stare seemed to drill into a point between my eyes.

"So, was that where he was murdered? In the parts shack?"

"Not sure yet. Maybe inside, maybe nearby." Westover looked off in the distance. "Don't suppose you have a security camera on your warehouse?"

I opened my mouth, but Dougie beat me to the punch.

"We do."

"You didn't mention that when we talked, Mr. Carstairs."

"You didn't ask."

OB glared at me, then Dougie. "I don't remember anyone consulting me about putting surveillance at the warehouse."

"The wildlife camera," Dougie said.

OB and Jenny nodded but Westover looked confused.

Dougie, OB, and I pulled up the app on our phones.

"Check CAM1 first," Dougie said. "It shows the front of the warehouse, the parts shack, and the workshop."

Westover looked over OB's shoulder and Jenny, over mine. It didn't take long to find the point when Natterly showed up and pried open the parts building door.

"Son of a bitch, he's going to rob me!" OB yelled. "Thieving bastard. I want him charged."

There was a moment of silence, but no one reminded OB that Natterly was dead.

Westover gestured at the phone. "Keep going."

We scanned through a few more minutes and a second man

arrived wearing clothes that looked garish even in the low-quality black-and-white video.

"Who's that?" Jenny asked.

"Matthew Tyson, the guy who called you about buying Hugh's land," OB said.

Tyson opened the door to the parts building and walked in, only to back out seconds later, practically nose-to-nose with Natterly.

"What's Natterly holding?" Dougie asked. "I can't tell because of the shadow from the tree."

We stopped the action so fingers could enlarge the image, but that only made the picture darker and less clear, so we went back to the wide view and hit play again.

Natterly advanced on Tyson, looming over him and holding the object in a threatening way. A kick to the groin sent Natterly to his knees and he ended in a face plant. With the upper hand, Tyson picked up the object Natterly dropped. When the sun glinted off of the metal, OB, Dougie, Jenny and I realized what it was.

"Oh, shit," OB said.

Jenny gasped.

"You don't think—" Dougie stopped, unable to complete the thought.

"What is that?" Westover asked. "It looks like the Jolly Green Giant's toenail clippers."

We ignored him and watched in stunned silence as Tyson struck Natterly. Repeatedly. Then he dropped the weapon and dragged the body out to the pasture behind the warehouse. He came back scuffing the ground in front of him, sending up plumes of dust.

"Destroying footprints and drag marks," Westover said.

Tyson picked up the bloody weapon and took it into the parts shack. When he came out, he was empty-handed and walked out of camera view.

"Now we know who killed Natterly," Dougie said.

"But why?" Jenny asked.

"Land," OB said. "Likely Hugh's. Natterly was talking about deeds. Maybe Tyson filed a fraudulent one, transferring Hugh's land to himself. Under a fake name, of course."

She looked dubious. "If Tyson did that, why ask me for a meeting to discuss selling him the land?"

"To find out how much you knew," Dougie said. "He shows you the fake backdated deed, and says, oops, just found this document. Your land isn't for sale because your uncle sold it before he died. If you accept that, he's home free. If you cry fraud, he could, under the same fake name, claim a land description error and withdraw his deed. No harm, no foul."

OB nodded. "Description mistakes happen all the time. All those numbers make it tricky."

"So where does Natterly come in?" Jenny asked.

I remembered the list of names and legal descriptions. "What if Natterly sold Tyson his tip list? Tyson filed the fake deed for Hugh's land. Natterly saw it and demanded money to keep quiet."

"Sounds like something Natterly would do," Dougie said. "Go on."

"Tyson refused to pay up, so Natterly went through with his threat and sent you a text saying you'd been cheated."

"Then he was stupid enough to tell Tyson what he'd done," OB said. "Makes sense."

At that point, Westover blew up. "That is all speculation."

To his surprise, I agreed with him. "It'll be easy to prove or disprove the theory. Check Hugh Miller's land record for a change of ownership."

Irritated, he asked a second time about the weapon Tyson used on Natterly.

Dougie ignored him. "At least Tyson didn't use it the way it was intended."

Jenny, OB, and I contemplated that sobering thought.

"Tyson probably didn't know what it was," OB said. "Which was fortunate."

"Is someone going to answer my question? What was that thing?" Westover asked.

Jenny, OB, and Dougie let me break the news. "It was a Burdizzo, a tool not used much anymore to, uh, obtain calf fries. It's not right for the small bulls we get, too heavy and hard to maneuver in a tight space. Knives are more precise."

For the second time that day, Westover's tan faded when he realized what I meant. He glanced over at Dougie and OB and the three men shared an uncomfortable look.

Jenny snickered and then looked chastened. "Poor Natterly. He was a jerk, but didn't deserve to be killed. Still, it could have been so much worse."

Even Westover agreed.

ACKNOWLEDGMENTS

As president of Partners in Crime, the San Diego chapter of Sisters in Crime, I'd like to thank a number of people for their hard work in helping us publish these outstanding stories in *Crime Under the Sun*. The result is a tribute to the two years of hard work you've put in. Our chapter really appreciates all you've done.

Carl Vonderau
President, 2022-2023

Barrie Summy and Kathy Krevat enthusiastically jumped on the anthology bandwagon. They recruited editors, managed a blind submission process and kept everyone on schedule through the selection and editing phase. They handled publicity and worked with the publisher to make sure this volume came out in its best form and on time.

Matt Coyle, Naomi Hirahara, and Tammy Kaehler took on the arduous task of reading just shy of 60 submissions and choosing the ones that would best fit together in this anthology. They also helped the authors revise their stories and make them even better.

Pat DiSandro provided outstanding copy editing.

Kim Keeline was an amazing go-to person for all things anthology-related. She was also a great help with publicity and cover suggestions.

Catriona McPherson wrote an excellent foreword that puts these stories in context with the theme of the anthology and entices readers to explore the work.

Art Taylor wrote a wonderful recommendation for our cover.

Down & Out Books, thank you for publishing our anthology and for arranging the terrific cover art.

For all the writers who submitted their work, we appreciate that you chose our anthology as a place where you would like your stories to appear.

A final thanks to our readers for supporting our chapter and these fine authors.

ABOUT THE EDITORS

MATT COYLE is the author of the bestselling Rick Cahill crime series. Matt knew he wanted to be a crime writer at age fourteen when his father gave him Raymond Chandler's *The Simple Art of Murder*. After finally seriously chasing that dream in his forties, it took Matt ten years to have his first mystery novel, *Yesterday's Echo*, published. It won the Anthony Award for Best Debut Mystery and the San Diego Book Award for Best Mystery. His subsequent books have been nominated for numerous awards and won, among them, the Shamus (twice), the Lefty, Authors on the Air Mystery and Book of the Year, the Ben Franklin Silver, and the Foreword Reviews Book of the Year Silver. Matt's books have also been named on many best of lists and in 2021, Matt was named the San Diego Writers Festival Mystery Writer of the Year. *Doomed Legacy* is his latest Rick Cahill crime novel and number ten, *Odyssey's End* comes out in December of this year. Matt lives in San Diego where he is writing his first standalone, which could blossom into a new series. You can learn more about him on his website: MattCoyleBooks.com.

NAOMI HIRAHARA is an Edgar Award-winning author of multiple traditional mystery series and noir short stories. Her Mas Arai mysteries feature a Los Angeles gardener and Hiroshima survivor who solves crimes. The Japanese translation of her seventh and final Mas Arai mystery, *Hiroshima Boy*, was nominated for two awards in Japan. Her first historical mystery is *Clark and Division*, which follows a Japanese American family's move to Chicago in 1944 after being released from a California wartime detention center. The book won a Bill Gottfried Memorial Lefty Award for Best Historical Mystery Novel; Simon & Schuster Mary Higgins Clark Award; and Macavity Award for Best Historical Mystery Novel. The follow-up to *Clark and Division*, *Evergreen*, will be released in August 2023. A former journalist with *The Rafu Shimpo* newspaper, Naomi has also written numerous non-fiction history books for both adults and young readers and curated exhibitions. She has also written a middle-grade novel, *1001 Cranes*. She received her bachelor's degree in international relations from Stanford University. She lives with her husband and over-affectionate rat terrier-chihuahua mix in Pasadena, California.

TAMMY KAEHLER is a writer, editor, project manager, and mystery author—as well as a racing fan and an appropriately enthusiastic cat lady. Mystery readers and racing insiders alike have praised the five books in her award-winning Kate Reilly Racing Mystery Series (*Dead Man's Switch*, *Braking Points*, *Avoidable Contact*, *Red Flags*, and *Kiss the Bricks*), which follows a young woman driver as she competes in races, advances in her career, and solves crimes in the racing world. One of Tammy's recent creative endeavors is a series of micro stories: creative and fun backstories for a local rescue's adoptable cats and kittens. She's also working on turning those stories and her experience fostering kittens into a new cozy mystery series. Tammy and her husband live in Southern California and share their lives with Pepper and Daisy, two feline siblings adopted through the rescue. Find out more at TammyKaehler.com.

ABOUT THE CONTRIBUTORS

SARAH BRESNIKER is a former librarian and paralegal who lives in Northern California with her husband and their sweet, lazy dog. She loves reading mysteries and exploring the natural beauty and fascinating history of the Monterey Peninsula. The immediate past president of the Capitol Crimes chapter of Sisters in Crime, her first short story was published in the 2021 Sisters in Crime Guppy Anthology and she is working on her first novel.

LYNNE BRONSTEIN is a veteran poet, fiction writer, and journalist. She has published five books, including *Nasty Girls* from Four Feathers Publishing. Her poetry and short fiction have appeared in everything from *Playgirl* to *Chiron Review*, from underground newspapers to National Public Radio. Her crime story "Mimo" appeared in SinC Los Angeles's 2017 anthology *LAst Resort*. She writes the column "Show Biz Cats," seen on Facebook. She loves film noir.

SHELLEY BURBANK is a mystery and women's fiction author and journalist based in Maine and San Diego, California. Her short fiction has been published in *True Story Magazine*, *San Diego Woman Magazine,* and *The Maine Review*. Her debut novel, *FINAL DRAFT: An Olivia Lively Mystery,* was published by Encircle Publications in March 2023. Learn more at

ShelleyBurbank.com.

WRONA GALL is a painter with a Master of Arts Degree whose years living and working in a former boiler factory in Chicago, surrounded by her bookie father-in-law's friends, inspired her to write fiction. Her work has appeared in museums from the Art Institute of Chicago to the San Diego Art Institute. Her short crime stories have appeared in the *Fire to Fly* anthology, SinC LA's *Last Resort* anthology, and SinC San Diego's *Crime Under the Sun* anthology. She also edited SinC *LA's Entertainment to Die For*.

B.J. GRAF lives in Los Angeles. In addition to five short stories ("Deus ex Machina," "Sandman," "Blood Shadows," "Shikata Ga Nai," and "Servants of the Place of Truth"), she has written one sci-fi-mystery novel, *Genesys X* (Fairwood Press), featuring the same detectives as three of her earlier stories. B.J. is also an Adjunct Professor who teaches Film and Classical Mythology at Pepperdine, UCLA, and CSUN. Previously, she worked as vice president of development for Abilene Pictures.

C.C. GUTHRIE's short stories have appeared in anthologies published by Wildside Press, Level Best Books, Superior Shores Press, Untreed Reads, and Camden Park Press. A member of Sisters in Crime, the SinC Guppy Chapter, the SinC San Diego Partners in Crime Chapter, and the Short Mystery Fiction Society, C.C. has been a Derringer finalist and a finalist for the Bill Crider Prize for Short Fiction.

A.P. JAMISON is a former investment banker who received her MFA from Columbia University. Her short stories, starring the intrepid detectives, Gus and Marshmallow, have appeared in MWA's 2022 Anthology, *Crime Hits Home,* and Malice Domestic's 2020 Anthology, *Mystery Most Theatrical.* Her first short story appeared in the Sisters in Crime/LA's 2019 Anthology—

Fatally Haunted. In 2018, she won the Sisters in Crime LA/MWA twelve-word story contest. She can be reached at AP-Jamison1025@gmail.com.

KATHY KINGSTON is a member of MWA and a former board member of SINCLA, where she was first published in their anthology, *Murder in LA-LA Land*, at the age of 66. More published stories followed in *King's River Life, Dark Moon Digest #5* and *The Lost Librarian's Grave.* She's from upstate New York and now resides in Venice, California, where she is an award-winning landscaper contractor specializing in drought tolerant landscapes.

KATHY KREVAT is the author of the bestselling Chocolate Covered Mystery series and the Gourmet Cat Mystery series. Her short story "One Flu Over the Cuckoo's Nest" was published in the *Crossing Borders* anthology. When she's not writing, Kathy performs stand-up comedy and tries very hard not to volunteer. Visit her at: KathyKrevat.com.

AXEL MILENS's short stories have been published in magazines and anthologies. He is a recipient of the Golden Fedora Fiction prize from Noir Nation. He recently completed his first novel, *10,000 Girls and One Ice Pick*, a humorous crime thriller to be published in 2023. Originally from Paris, France, he currently resides in the Hollywood hills with his wife, two evil teenagers and an old gassy dog. AxelMilens.com.

JOHN EDWARD MULLEN is the award-winning author of *Digital Dick* in which an Artificial Intelligence investigates a murder. In his latest novel, *Nell: Marshal of Bodie*, eighteen-year-old, one-legged Nell Doherty dreams of becoming a Pinkerton detective in 1892 California. First, though, she must take her father's place as Marshal, and—with the help of her half-Irish, half-Chinese best friend—track down the desperadoes who shot him. John is currently writing a sequel, *Nell: Pinkerton Detective.*

KATHY NORRIS writes books featuring people of color in settings ranging from the Great Depression to the recent Covid-19 pandemic. Two of her short stories are included in Sisters in Crime anthologies. She is currently working on a detective series featuring an African American Vietnam War veteran battling PTSD. Kathy lives in Los Angeles but loves to wander. Next up: an expedition to Antarctica...even though she hates to be cold!

MICHELLE RODENBORN is a 2022 Claymore Award Finalist—Thriller category—for her debut novel, *Scream at Center Ring*. The crime thriller was informed and inspired by her experiences working in the Los Angeles Criminal Courts, first as a trial attorney in the Public Defender's Office, followed by a six-year stint sitting as an L.A. Superior Court Judge Pro Tem. Michelle is a member of the National and Los Angeles chapters of Sisters in Crime.

WENDALL THOMAS teaches in the Graduate Film School at UCLA, lectures internationally on screenwriting, and has worked as an entertainment reporter, development executive, script consultant, and film and television writer, including a stint on PBS's *Wishbone*. Her short fiction has appeared in the crime anthologies *Ladies Night*, *Last Resort*, and *Murder-A-Go-Gos*. The fourth book in her Anthony-, Macavity-, and Lefty-nominated Cyd Redondo series is due to be published in the spring of 2023. She lives in Los Angeles.

JAMES THORPE's father was a mortician, and his mother played the accordion, so even at a tender young age James realized he was destined to become either a serial killer or a writer. Splitting the difference, he began his Emmy Award-winning career in advertising, eventually leading him to Hollywood where he now writes and produces for television and film. James is a proud member of MWA, ITW, CWA, and SinC, and rarely wakes up screaming anymore.

On the following pages are a few
more great titles from the
Down & Out Books publishing family.

For a complete list of books and to
sign up for our newsletter,
go to DownAndOutBooks.com.

ANDREW NETTE

Orphan Road
A Chance Novel
Andrew Nette

Down & Out Books
May 2023
978-1-64396-315-0

Professional thief Gary Chance is drawn into a scheme by his former employer, Vera Leigh, to save her failing Melbourne S&M club by retrieving a stash of diamonds allegedly stolen as part of one of Australia's biggest heists.

But they're not the only ones looking.

The heist always goes wrong and the consequences, even half a century later, can be deadly.

Gallows Dome
Nolan Knight

Down & Out Books
June 2023
978-1-64396-317-4

Lena Madadhi is desperate, a middle-aged L.A. arts teacher whose teen daughter has been abducted.

When seeking help from a private investigator, Joe Delancey, she finds he's on a case at a Central Valley truck stop, undercover among truckers and nomads in a doomsday sect called *Gallows Dome*.

The further she digs to find Joe, the closer she comes to hell, salvation and…her beloved daughter.

Because the Night
A Henry Malone Novel
James D.F. Hannah

Down & Out Books
June 2023
978-1-64396-318-1

Henry Malone finds himself under two distinct forms of pressure: He's running for sheriff of Parker County, and he's trying to find a pregnant woman's missing ex-con boyfriend.

But after a violent encounter leaves a friend near death, Henry discovers a series of betrayals and double crosses that climax with a deadly assault against a band of criminals with nothing to lose.

A Semblance of Control
Mark T. Conard

Down & Out Books
June 2023
978-1-64396-302-0

One night Jake Micallef does a little breaking-and-entering and stumbles upon a plot to assassinate his estranged brother, who just happens to be the Mayor of New York City.

As Jake wrestles with that bombshell, another one walks straight into his life: Marcie Yates. Marcie eerily resembles Jake's old girlfriend, the woman who helped his brother tear his world apart. But when thugs kidnap Marcie to keep Jake from interfering in the assassination plot, he has no choice but to track down the conspirators, only to discover he's fallen right into their trap. In the end, Jake must risk everything to save Marcie and stop the bullet headed for his brother.

Made in the USA
Monee, IL
21 July 2023